AGE OF ICE

FATED SERIES BOOK TWO

MARIAH STONE

Stone
Publishing

GET A FREE MARIAH STONE BOOK!

Join Mariah's mailing list to be the first to know of new releases, free books, special prices, and other author giveaways.

freehistoricalromancebooks.com

ALSO BY MARIAH STONE

Mariah's Time travel Romance Series

- CALLED BY A HIGHLANDER
- CALLED BY A VIKING
- CALLED BY A PIRATE
- FATED

Mariah's Regency Romance Series

- DUKES AND SECRETS

View all of Mariah's Books in Reading Order

Scan the QR code for the complete list of Mariah's ebooks, paperbacks, and audiobooks in reading order.

One day long ago
    my life was already shaped,
    and my fate was fixed.
    —Unknown, *The Poetic Edda: Stories of the Norse Gods
and Heroes*

ONE

Norway, 896

THE SHED REEKED of old fish. They must have cleaned out herring and salmon guts here, Ella thought, right on that massive wooden table. Even in semidarkness, scales stuck to the scarred surface glimmered dully with silver and mother-of-pearl.

The only light came during the day. Dust danced in the sunrays seeping through the uneven slits between the poorly constructed wall planks and falling on the only three pieces of furniture. One, Ella's amazing bed, otherwise known as a heap of straw in the corner. Two, the aforementioned stinking table set against the opposite wall. Three, a stool with three uneven legs.

During the three days that she'd been trapped here, she'd tried to move the table so that it stood next to the door. Her plan had been to climb on top of it and attack the guard or King Harald himself. That was pretty much her only chance to escape since her gun and her Kevlar vest had been taken away from her.

But the damn table was like a boulder and just wouldn't budge.

There were no windows, not even a floor—just cold, packed dirt—and plenty of gaps in the walls.

And there was the door.

Her only way out.

Her only way to go back to her own time...or at least a chance to find out how to return home. Because she wasn't even entirely sure how she'd ended up here in the first place. All she knew was that one moment she'd been in the Port of Boston, standing in a warehouse among dozens of wounded and dead bodies, cocaine bags, and a giant golden spindle that was a broken time machine.

The man she was falling for had just told her two things. He'd called her his love.

And he'd told her he'd smuggled a goddamn nuclear reactor to power the time machine.

She'd gotten mad at him. She'd said things... She'd touched the golden spindle and...*poof*.

When she'd opened her eyes, she'd been standing on a cliff overlooking a Norwegian fjord, a long, narrow inlet flanked by mountains. And King Harald and a band of his Viking warriors had immediately taken her captive.

Ella pressed her face to a slit between the planks. Even through the gap, she could see the breathtaking, rough beauty of the place. The village was on the shore of a fjord with cliffs on both sides that shot up like granite walls, so high they could support the sky.

The houses themselves were all made of timber. None of them had windows and all of them had thatched roofs with carved dragon gables. Most of the women were blond and wore apron dresses, and the men wore linen and woolen tunics and some sort of baggy trousers and patched shoes.

Goats, sheep, chickens, and geese walked around. Dogs barked, children ran and played. Men cut firewood, carried buckets of water, dressed fish and game. Women were mostly indoors, no doubt cooking, though Ella saw several sweep and clean, take out buckets with food waste for the pigs and cows, and run after the children. She heard everything from outside the shed really well, and still didn't know how she could understand Old Norse without ever learning it.

There was always a guard by her door, one of the Viking warriors. She'd seen them when they opened the door and let the slave girl, Ciara, in to bring her food and take her night pot out.

King Harald himself hadn't come to see her yet, and she'd overheard people talking, saying he was away.

She'd like to punch Harald in the face. How long was he intending to keep her here—and why? Harald was the one who had sent those Viking assassins after Channing through time...

Channing...

How could a single word send a stabbing pain through her, as though a needle pierced right through the middle of her chest?

Every single doubt about him had vanished. He'd been telling the truth this whole time.

Time travel was real.

Any thoughts she'd had about this being a trick had been wiped away by the three days she'd spent observing people, listening to conversations about raids, fishing, the harvest. About the blacksmith being too cocky and asking prices that were too high—two sacks of barley for a sword. The worries about an unknown illness that had made an old man weak and double up in pain. How a woman had lost her baby in child-birth, but thankfully, was alive herself.

The talk about making mead, and the blot—a ritual sacrifice of a sheep on one of the rune rocks—that was planned for King Harald's return.

At first, she'd thought this might be some sort of reenact-ment game...a role-play...some secluded community that had gone hardcore on the whole "let's live in the past" thing.

But she wasn't even in the United States anymore.

Channing had been telling the truth... He had been just trying to get back to the age where he belonged.

This age.

The wrong age for her.

She had to find a way back to the twenty-first century.

Time stretched and crawled, endless and merciless. On the fourth day, horse hooves and heavy steps sounded from the outside. Many excited voices approached, and then the door opened, letting direct sunlight in shielded by several tall, broad-shouldered, muscular frames.

She jumped to her feet, her knees bent, her fists clenched, ready to fight if she needed to.

One of the shadows entered, and as he stepped inside, she noticed his red hair and beard, his handsome, intelligent face. King Harald.

"Stay back," he threw over his shoulder. "She is not a threat to me."

He was wearing a long bear-fur hide on his shoulders that gave him even more mass and presence. He turned back and, using his ax, pushed the door closed.

Why were all these men so huge? Channing was big, but many men in the village looked like they had tree trunks for arms and boulders for shoulders. Must be all the longship rowing. Even the king looked like a weathered warrior.

Well, he clearly wore more expensive outfits. The bear cloak was probably special, and she wondered if he had hunted the animal himself. And he wore silver chains and a thick torc—a large, rigid ring made of silver strands twisted together—around his neck.

And then there was this look in his eyes. She'd seen it many times. All men in power had it. That calm, contained arrogance, the sense that they owned everything. Channing had it, too, only behind it, there was a big, kind heart and an unbendable sense of honor.

Harald turned to her, then put his ax into the belt around his waist. "So. Gods sent you to me through time."

She raised one eyebrow. "Not sure about the 'gods' part, but definitely through time. And you will help me to go back."

He chuckled and little wrinkles formed around his eyes. "I will do no such thing, woman."

Anger that she'd been containing for the past four days started boiling somewhere deep in her guts. "How dare you." Her voice came out low, but the smirk in his eyes was gone as he, no doubt, heard the steel beneath her words.

"How dare I?" He walked farther into the shed, the streams of sunlight sparkling off his chain mail under his bearskin. "I am king. I am the favorite of the gods. I dare everything."

He stopped before the pile of hay in the corner.

"You cocky son of a bitch. You know that what you did was kidnapping, a punishable offense in my time? Had you done that in Boston, you'd be in jail faster than you could take your next breath."

Harald cocked one brow, amusement returning into his gaze. "I do not know what a jail is or a punishable offense, but I like the fire in you, woman."

"Stop calling me 'woman,'" she growled.

"Are you not a woman?" His gaze went up and down her body, and Ella stopped a shiver of disgust.

"I am, but that doesn't make any difference for—"

He crossed the distance between them in three steps. One moment, he was across the room, the next he was towering over her like a giant bear.

"Oh, Freya's tongue, it makes all the difference." He raised his hand and dragged his knuckle down her cheek. With her stomach in knots, Ella shook his hand off. All humor from his face gone, he grabbed her cheeks between his thumb and his index finger in a painful pinch, squishing her lips together. "The Norns send women across time to men so that they find love. Mia, Hakon Ulfson's wife, is a time traveler. There are others. I have concubines, slaves I use for pleasure. I have children, though currently not a wife. But I do not love any of them. Who is to say you were not sent here for me?"

A cold shiver swept through Ella. She was so far out of her depth here. This time was so different. Women had fought for centuries for the right to be as independent as men, to be their equals.

The Viking Age was just at the beginning of that fight. Which meant, this jerk and other men like him treated women like property.

Oh, hell no. She wouldn't let anyone treat her with anything but respect, and she'd show him.

She stomped on his foot. He let go of her face and groaned in pain. Using his distraction, she threw her elbow back and drove her fist into his stomach, only to meet a steely wall of muscle. His next grunt sounded like a chuckle.

She'd show him.

"I'll teach you to treat women with respect."

Using his distraction, she kneed him right between the legs.

He made a strange sound like a loud sigh and stepped back, doubling up and covering his groin.

"You bitch," he gave out.

"I am not a wallflower, nor a slave, nor an object of amusement for anyone, not even a king. I am a police officer, the daughter of a police officer, and I have a sick father, and a brother with special needs, and a whole family that depends on me. I eat scumbags like you for breakfast. And if you touch me like that ever again, next time your balls won't hurt because I kicked them, but because you'll be missing them."

Harald exhaled slowly and straightened himself. He must still be in a lot of pain behind the reddening stone mask of his face. Somewhere deep, a small voice told her she was probably wrong to make an enemy out of him. Told her she would be better off being sly and diplomatic.

He cleared his throat, his eyes fixed on her. "I will treat you with respect, woman. I always treat women with respect. You are no slave and you are a warrior woman, I see. But if you think I will back off, you are wrong. If anything, your strength and your beauty makes me want you more."

Her jaw must have hit the ground. "Why do you even need me? Why are you keeping me here?"

Slowly, he stepped towards her, his mouth tight in pain. "You are so beautiful...It is hard to imagine Freya herself did not come down from Valhalla."

She swallowed, fighting the instinct to back away from him. When another Viking had towered over her like that, she'd wanted to kiss him, to hug him, to dissolve in his touch.

She wanted to run away from this man. "What do you want from me?"

"If you are from the future, you might have heard of Ulf Hakonson?"

He was speaking of Channing, using his Norse name, Ulf.

"Not just him. I know your goons, Eirik, Ragnar, and Náli."

His eyes didn't just widen, they sparkled. "Did Ulf's death save the world, just as the völva foretold?"

Her heart slammed against her ribs. She should think carefully, she should play this right. But the memory of the swords and axes flashing, hurting Channing, of her aiming her gun. Her bullet, piercing Eirik. The first life she'd ever taken. Blood flowing.

The cool, smooth surface of the time machine under her palm...and then nothing.

All because of him.

"No, you murderous bastard. Your assassins died. Ulf is still alive."

"And you saw all that?"

"Yes, I saw all that. I killed Eirik."

Harald's face relaxed in a serene, peaceful expression that made the skin on her back crawl. "Then the answer to your question of why you are here is clear, beautiful woman from the future."

"Oh yeah?" She didn't want to know the answer. She shouldn't ask, she shouldn't even bother. But like an idiot, she asked, "Why?"

"Because you will bring him to me. And when I kill him and stop Ragnarök, you will be mine."

TWO

Boston, 2021

THE METAL BARS of the jail rattled and Channing raised his head.

Detective Ricardo Sanchez appeared in the corridor behind the bars, his eyes two hard pieces of obsidian. "Hakonson, you have a visitor."

Channing stood up from the bench. His stomach was in knots, worry for Ella burning his guts like acid. He'd been here since yesterday, but his lawyer hadn't managed to get him out yet.

On the way here from the port, Ricardo had glared at him in the rearview mirror but said nothing. A jail medic had looked at the cut on Channing's shoulder, which had been left by Eirik's sword. He'd put some glue on it and dressed it, declaring it was minor. The wound on his other shoulder left by Ragnar's ax several days ago was aching. Seeing it had been dressed already, the medic hadn't even looked at it. There were way too many offenders waiting for an examination with far worse wounds, bad frostbite, and illnesses that had flared up due to the lack of medical support and shortage of medicine in the city.

Yesterday, a proper battle had taken place in Channing's secret laboratory. The police had attacked the Mafia who had smuggled cocaine along with Channing's nuclear reactor. Meanwhile, the three Viking assassins sent by King Harald to kill him and stop Ragnarök had decided the ensuing chaos was their best bet to accomplish their mission by capturing Ella. He'd had to kill two of them, and Ella had saved his life by shooting and killing Eirik.

And then, she'd touched the broken time machine...and disappeared.

"Did you find her?" asked Channing, even though he knew she had traveled through time.

But a small part of him was holding out hope that she hadn't, that something else had happened in the warehouse to explain her disappearance.

Or that she'd managed to return.

Metal jiggled as Ricardo unlocked the cell door and let it slide to the side. "Turn around."

Channing turned his back and hard metal bit into his wrists as Ricardo put the handcuffs on.

"No news?" asked Channing.

"Shut up. Go."

So, no news. As Channing walked down the dingy hall painted in a sickly pastel yellow, he could feel Sanchez's eyes practically boring holes into the back of his skull.

"You know I want to find her as much as you do."

"Shut up, you fucking bastard."

There was so much rage, so much hatred in his voice... Ricardo cared about her. And not just as a work partner.

Channing suspected there was much, much more to how Ricardo felt about Ella... So much more that jealousy stung Channing. Well, good. Maybe if Channing couldn't convince Ricardo to let him go on a logical level, he could on an emotional level. Channing was the only one who could save Ella now, the only one who could bring her back.

As Ricardo opened the door to an office, Channing's stomach dropped. Bryan O'Connor, Ella's father, and Ted, her half brother, sat at the desk.

"What is Ted doing here?" Channing glanced back into the corridor where two cops led a massive man in handcuffs somewhere.

Ricardo pushed Channing forward and closed the door behind him. "I wonder the same thing."

"How the hell is this place good for a kid to visit?" growled Channing. "Do you think Ella would have allowed this?"

Bryan scowled at Channing. "No, she wouldn't have liked this one bit."

Ricardo gestured at the chair by the desk, and Channing sat down. Ricardo stood next to the desk, his arms crossed over his chest.

The office was small and cluttered. Stacks of paper and thick manila folders lay on every file cabinet in the room. A house plant was slowly dying on the windowsill under the half-lowered blinds. Sad gray daylight seeped through the snowed-in window.

"Hi, Ted," said Channing. "Hello, Bryan."

"Hello, Channing!" said Ted. "Dad doesn't want me here."

"I can't imagine why," said Ricardo. "What the— Why, Bryan?"

Bryan's jaw muscles worked. "Gloria has a cleaning job and she can't miss it. And I...I have to know where my daughter is. I'm a cop, even though I'm retired. I know you have the answer to what happened to her. And I can't wait until Captain Wilson can spare enough officers to look for her. The police are barely able to keep up as it is, and it's getting worse. What is a missing cop to him when the whole world is tumbling down into chaos? I have to take matters into my own hands."

"And I do, too!" Ted proclaimed. "I'll help find Ella."

Channing's heart dropped to his feet. He knew his own family must have felt a similar desperation and determination even though they knew perfectly well where he'd disappeared to.

Ricardo shifted his weight without untangling his arms.

"So," Bryan said. "Will you help me? Help me find my daughter. I know you care about her, too." He cleared his throat. "I suspect it was your anonymous donation that got me into that experimental cancer treatment program at Mass Gen."

Ricardo opened his mouth, but Bryan shot a glance at him. "You didn't hear anything."

Ricardo took one step forward, his arms falling to his sides. "You have cancer?"

"What is cancer?" said Ted, and Bryan sighed.

"It's like a game," said Bryan.

A game with death, all right.

Ted blinked. "Oh. Will it let us find Ella?"

Ricardo sighed. "God, I hope not. Look, Bryan, I asked the witnesses, the wounded cops who were conscious enough to see what happened, and the scientists. It all checks out. She touched that damned golden thing and just poof...she was gone." He looked at Channing. "I don't know what you did to her to make her disappear into thin air when she touched that thing—a secret trap door or something, maybe—but I know you're responsible."

Ricardo didn't fool Channing. Behind the big-boned, goofy

exterior was a sharp mind. Ricardo had chosen his mask well, and Channing knew all about wearing masks. He'd worn the mask of a modern man since he'd traveled to the twenty-first century fourteen years ago, at the age of eighteen. A Viking in the modern world. His whole life had changed.

"I care about Ella more than you know," Channing said through a throat that felt full of gravel. "And I think I can find out where she went."

Bryan exhaled sharply. "Tell me everything."

Time travel sounded like a thing of magic and myth to most people. Cops especially would have a hard time believing him. But he had to take the risk of sounding crazy. His main goal was to find Ella and to get her back home, to her family. And who else would be a better ally than her own father?

He leaned forward. "I know it sounds insane, but I was researching time travel." He glanced at Ricardo, who came a stop closer to the table. "I hired two MIT scientists and they built me a time machine. We were about to launch it, and I was about to go through time, but then the Mafia came, and the police arrived, too. What I think happened was that Ella went through time instead of me."

Silence fell on their table. He could imagine Bryan's and Ricardo's internal voices laughing at him.

Ted was the only one who was looking at him with concentrated reflection. "Ella took a trip to a different time?"

"You have got to be kidding me..." murmured Ricardo.

Bryan cleared his throat and sighed out. His knobby fingers curled into a fist. "Can you prove it's true?"

Ricardo gasped. "Bryan, you're not serious. Don't you realize what he's doing? He's trying to smooth-talk himself out of getting locked up for kidnapping! *Time travel?* He's a drug smuggler, and a smuggler of illegal nuclear materials! And he's responsible for your daughter's disappearance. Come on!"

Ted glared at Ricardo, his eyebrows a single straight line. "You're being mean."

"Sorry, Ted. I don't mean to be. All I want is to find your sister."

"I think all of us here agree on that," said Bryan.

Ricardo made a wide, swiping gesture with his arm. "So you believe him?"

Bryan's jaw tightened. "I don't know. Time travel is a hard thing to buy. But people believed the world was flat before we knew it was a globe. At one point, we didn't think we could cross oceans. Or fly. Or go to space." His chest rose and fell quicker. "It's very likely I do not have much time. And I'll be damned if I don't try to get my baby girl back to safety by whatever means possible."

Ted frowned at his father. "Why do you not have much time, Dad?"

Bryan ruffled Ted's hair, his eyes watering. "I have plenty of time, son. All my time for you, your mom, and your sister. We just need to find her." Then he looked at Ricardo and tapped his index finger on the surface of the table, and Channing saw the same look of a determined warrior that he'd seen every time his own father gathered his troops to fight against an enemy or protect Lomdalen against raiders. "Find her. If not us, no one will."

Ricardo let out a long sigh. "I'll most likely regret this, but our best bet is to go back to the last place she was seen. The place where she disappeared in a puff of smoke."

Ted's eyes widened. "Like a faerie? Is Ella a faerie?"

Channing didn't know about being a faerie, but he suspected Ella could do more than anyone was aware of. And, perhaps, even more than she knew herself. The time machine had been broken. It wouldn't work for him or the scientists. So what power had made it function for her?

"No, Ted," said Channing. "Ella is your sister who you've known all your life and who loves you very much. There are things we don't understand, but that's why your dad, your uncle Ricardo, and I, we'll find her."

"How could this have happened?" asked Ricardo. "If she did...time travel...instead of you or whatever...do you know where to? And how can we get her back?"

Channing nodded. "The settings were set to 896, Lomdalen, Norway. That was where I was supposed to go."

"Why?" asked Ricardo in disbelief.

"I have a...personal interest." It was, perhaps, too much for one talk, to both reveal he was a time traveler born in another century, and that he wanted to go back to his family.

"Is that...the Middle Ages? The Viking Age?" asked Bryan.

Channing bit his upper lip, tension in his whole body rising. "Yes."

Bryan squinted at him in confusion. "Ella's mother was obsessed with Vikings, Norse mythology. She did embroidery as masterful as real paintings. I've always thought it was an eccentric interest of hers, but when she left, I did wonder where she'd disappeared to...and how could she have not left any trace. We weren't legally married, we just lived together. After she left, I realized she had no Social Security number, no passport, nothing. There are no records of her existence."

Ricardo blinked. "I didn't know that."

Bryan scratched his head. "Yeah."

"I mean, I knew Ella was looking for her mom who'd left her, and Wilson was mad she'd used police resources for personal reasons. Now I know why she took that chance—with no records and no trace to follow, the police databases were likely her only hope of finding her mom."

"Norway. Viking Age. Somehow, it makes sense," Bryan mumbled as if he hadn't been listening to Ricardo at all.

Channing knew he was close to convincing them. Most importantly, Ricardo. "I can go there and get her. I'll make sure she returns here. To all of you."

Ricardo pivoted towards Channing and towered over him, his hands on his hips. "How?"

"Take me to the spindle. Get me the scientists, Munchie and Georgina. They send me there, and I find her."

"Is Ella with Vikings?" asked Ted. "The guys with horns on their hats? Like Rolf?"

Rolf was a superhero from the comic books based on Norse mythology that Ted adored.

Channing nodded. "Yes. They don't have hats with horns, but otherwise, yes."

"Aren't they rapists and raiders?" whispered Bryan.

Channing sighed. "No. Some of them are, but so are people everywhere. Prisons are full of them."

Ricardo shook his head and leaned on the table. "Look, I'm not saying I believe you, but I do see the point of going back to where she disappeared and figuring out what happened."

Channing said, "So get me there."

Ricardo's head hung between his shoulders, and he didn't say anything for several long moments. When he looked at Channing again, his mouth was curved down like he'd tasted something bitter. "Okay. Get her back."

Channing knew he was about to make the third oath in his life that was bigger than him. The first one had been his loyalty to his father, Jarl Hakon, which meant he acknowledged him as his lord and would fight for him to the death. The second one was to Ella, to be loyal to her and never betray her trust.

This would be his third one. To Bryan, Ted, and Ricardo. And this one might bring him his end, but it didn't matter. Nothing mattered more than Ella. "I swear on my life I will bring her home."

THREE

The steam rising from the stew tickled Ella's nose. It was a strong-tasting meat that must be some sort of game, oats, peas, and unidentifiable root vegetables turned gray through the long cooking. No salt, no pepper.

Ciara had also brought a piece of freshly grilled salmon, but Ella had practically gulped that thing down, barely minding the bones. That had been heaven. The stew wasn't great, but it was food and Ella needed strength. During the last couple of days, she had been fed once a day, and most of the time it was something overcooked or simple boiled parsnips and dried salted or smoked fish. Bread had been pretty much impossible to eat. It was tough, and Ella suspected sawdust was mixed into it.

With only Ciara visiting her, and the outside world being visible through the slits in the wall, Ella's mood had deteriorated. She hadn't seen King Harald since his last visit two days ago, and she hadn't been outside at all.

Every day, her hope of returning to the twenty-first century, to her family, shrank. She understood how Channing must have felt being stuck in modern times.

How were her father, Ted and Gloria, and the rest of her family? She'd seen them every day for as long as she could remember, and she missed them. Dad's hard, steely eyes, Gloria's sweet fussing in the mornings as she made coffee, fried eggs, and bacon and yelled for everyone to hurry to the kitchen. Ted switching on the radio in the kitchen at exactly eight o'clock to listen to the news, which had been so bad recently that Ella usually switched it back off at 8:02.

There were no sleepy hugs smelling of Ted's still-sweet child's morning breath, no discussions with Dad at the dinner table about her recent cases, no warnings from Gloria for Ella to be careful out there, not to take unnecessary risks.

No warm house, creaky and old, smelling like aged wood, and like shepherd's pie, and like her childhood. No footsteps and voices coming from upstairs as Uncle Maurice, Aunt Cara, and their daughter, Fiona, went around the house. Often, their son, Rob, his pregnant wife, Stella, and their toddler, Pamela, joined them from the third floor of the triple-decker, and the huge family would talk, fuss, laugh, argue, have friends and neighbors over.

And they all depended on her paycheck.

If she stayed here any longer, the police may soon assume her dead and stop paying her salary. They'd lose the house. Where would they go during the coldest winter in history, and while the world was tumbling down a steep slope towards its demise?

But none of that was clear here. In the ninth century, as far as Ella could say, everything was fine. Winter hadn't come yet. There were no wolves chasing people, no civil unrest, no earthquakes, no storms, or anything that would alarm people about the coming of Ragnarök.

And Channing wasn't here.

His absence was a hole in the middle of her chest, aching, throbbing.

This loneliness and silence, being trapped in the dark shack, made her edgy. Ciara was the only person she'd seen in days, and the girl was wary of her.

Ciara covered the straw with a grayish-yellow piece of fabric that, based on stains and small tears, had seen some use. Back in the twenty-first century, Ella would never sleep on something like that. Now, it looked inviting.

"Ye're nae from this time, are ye?"

It was so unexpected, Ella wasn't even sure she'd heard her right. Ciara spoke Old Norse with a Scottish accent... an odd combination. Ciara had been this quiet, somber presence, just bringing food, cleaning the bed. Ella had tried to talk to her, but the girl had given her one-syllable answers.

Ciara looked down on her feet. "What was I thinking? Forgive me..."

Ella felt sorry for her and didn't want to lose this thread of human connection. Or was this the beginning of Stockholm syndrome?

"How do you know?" she asked.

Ciara straightened, her intelligent brown eyes meeting Ella's. "I heard things..."

Without replying, Ella returned to her bowl. She liked the woman, but she wasn't sure if it was safe to admit things like time travel.

Ciara continued in an even quieter voice. "And I ken things..."

"What things?"

Although at first Ella had thought Ciara was a teenager, with her thin body and sharp elbows, Ella had soon realized she wasn't that young. She must be older than Ella, based on those wrinkles and deep, dark circles around Ciara's eyes. She might be malnourished. And her hands were hardened from too much work, the knuckles thick, skin red and cracked, and she had age spots on the backs of her hands.

"I ken enough to say ye may be nae from this time..."

Ella put the bowl she was half drinking, half eating from on the fishy table. "Did Harald say that?"

"Oh, aye. How ye appeared out of nowhere in front of him on the cliff... But..."

Ciara fingered her rough, homespun apron dress, which was rugged and dirty and had more patches than Ella could count. Her brown eyes were shiny, and her brown hair hung loose in ragged, tangled locks that looked like wasps' nests.

"But what?"

"But 'tis nae the first story of travel through the river of time that I ken."

Something within Ella quivered, reminded of her dreams. She'd wondered why she hadn't gotten them in a while—her strange dreams where she had been able to pause and unpause time, change things a little.

She'd never heard anyone talk about time travel apart from Channing. And now, Ciara. "River of time?" Ella asked. "What do you mean? How do you even know all this?"

"I..." She straightened up, leaving Ella's mattress on the ground, and fumbling with her hands in front of her. "I shouldna even talk with you about this. I should just do my work and leave."

But she didn't. Instead, she stood as though waiting for something. As with suspects and informants, Ella sensed a readiness to talk. Sometimes they kept a secret for so long, they craved to let it out to a listening ear that wouldn't judge. That might understand.

"How long have you been here, Ciara?" asked Ella, turning on her stool to face the woman.

"Half my life..." Ciara looked at her feet, still playing with her hands.

"Where are you from?"

"I'm from the kingdom of Alba, mistress. The islands the Vikings call Sutherland. Fifteen or so winters ago, dragonships came to the shore that I had called home. I had just been promised to a lad in my village when they came. Burned half of the village and took all the women and lasses that lived through the raid. They sold most, and sold me to King Harald. He wasna king back then, just a jarl. I've been here ever since."

Alba... Sutherland... All that was Scotland back then.

Ciara swallowed and looked down at her hands, as though she were responsible for someone grabbing her and kidnapping her.

Ella had never had to deal with human trafficking, but she'd heard stories from colleagues who'd worked on busting a sex-slave network that brought girls from Eastern Europe and Mexico to Boston and other towns in New England.

She needed to be extremely careful not to scare Ciara away. "The police...where I work...we fight against that."

Ciara's eyes widened. "Ye fight against thralldom?"

Ella caught Ciara's eyes. "Yes. We fight against rape, we fight against injustice, we fight against racism, discrimination... against all crimes."

"Ye canna fight it in this time. 'Tis what Vikings...pirates... do. They raid, they take thralls. 'Tis how they get their masterful ships made, iron armor and weapons forged, sails woven for their expeditions. They raid in the Isles, in Northumbria and Sussex, in Alba, and among the Baltic tribes."

She was furious on Ciara's behalf and that of all others

taken against their will. But, although painful to hear, Ella wasn't surprised. Most of the time, the victims of human trafficking were broken, traumatized so that they didn't even consider trying to escape. Often, the punishment was a severe beating or death. Ella had heard about only one victim who'd managed to break free, but she developed a dissociative identity disorder. How was it, for someone to live a life where it was a completely normal thing to be a slave?

"What do you do as a slave?"

Ciara's shoulders slumped. She picked up a bucket with water and a wet cloth and scrubbed the table. "Anything." Her voice was void. Empty. "Clean. Wash. Make beds. Help with cooking. Make the lord happy."

Ella's stomach churned. "What do you mean, make the lord happy?"

Ciara plunged the cloth into the water. "If the king tells me to warm his bed, I oblige."

Ella's skin crawled. "Damn it."

Weakly, Ciara slapped the wet cloth onto the table and moved it over the surface. "A thrall is nothing. A thrall doesna even count as a concubine. A thrall is a thing one owns. Like a horse. The king tells a horse to walk. It does. The king tells me to spread my legs. I do."

Ella's whole being chilled. She laid her hand on Ciara's shoulder. "Please, stop, Ciara. Let me do this for you."

Ciara looked at her, and illuminated by the weak sunlight, her face looked like a skull, like she was already dead and only made herself move.

Ciara straightened. "Doesna matter, mistress. Ye remind me of my sister. I shouldna care about ye, about anyone, really. But I do. I dinna want ye to end up in my position tomorrow."

Ella's feet tingled like they had been plunged into a bucket full of nails. "I won't. And I'll help you get out of here before it's too late for you."

Ciara rubbed the table with the cloth, and dirty gray water dripped between the planks onto the dirt-packed floor. "There's nae other life than this."

Ella grabbed Ciara's arms and straightened her up, looking into her eyes. Ciara's gaze was empty and unfocused.

Ella grasped her hand. "Don't say that. Please. Surely there's a way to escape or...do something."

Ciara shook her head. "Ye dinna ken. Ye ken nothing. The lives I took..."

"What do you mean? Did you have to kill someone in self-defense?"

She shook her head. "The lives I took were innocent..."

Innocent... "Abortions?"

She nodded. "There are herbs, but the healer gives them to the important women in the village first. I'd like a bairn, but I dinna want a child to be born into this. A lass would most likely be killed right away. A lad may live, but he would be a slave. So I go to the conjure woman and she takes care of it. Although the king would kill both me and her if he kent I rid myself of his bairns. Slaves are nae allowed to make decisions like that."

Ella closed her eyes and shook her head as horror dripped in her stomach in a cold trickle. The sex slavery cartels she'd heard of had condoms, but they also used misoprostol, the "morning after" pill, which was also an antiulcer medication, that caused abortions.

Ciara whispered, "Sometimes I wish I had died with my family... Every bairn I lost took a part of my soul with them. I dinna ken if there's anything left."

To hell with those Viking bastards. To hell with the men who thought it was okay to own another human being.

"Ciara..." Ella hugged her by the shoulders, ignoring the

scent of her unwashed body. She had a sense she was hugging an empty vessel.

Perhaps Ciara had surrendered.

But perhaps Ella could still help her.

Ella was no one's slave, and she wouldn't let any woman be a slave. She just had to find a way out. Harald clearly wasn't going to help her get back home, so she'd have to find another way.

"How do you know about time travel?" asked Ella.

"'Tis an old Pictish story. A faerie has lost the love of her life and always searches for a way to make humans meet the loves of their lives."

Ella shook her head. "Okay. But what about King Harald? He said something about a Norn?"

"Oh, aye. A völva, which means a seeress, a witch, heard the Norn's prophecy. She came to King Harald while he was in Lomdalen with Jarl Hakon and told him he needed to kill Ulf, the jarl's son. Norns are the three most powerful beings. They rule the lives of the mortals and the gods. They say one of the Norns has a particular joy of seeing humans travel through time and find their destinies. Just like that Highland faerie."

Like Mia, Channing's mother, who was born in the twentieth century, but traveled in time to the ninth century where she found the love of her life, and gave birth to Channing, who was supposed to live in the twenty-first century.

But Channing, born in the ninth century, but living in the twenty-first century from the age of eighteen, just wanted to get back to his family.

And now, Ella...

Born in the twentieth century.

A prisoner to Harald in the ninth. Surely this couldn't be her destiny. She wouldn't be kept against her will by Harald or by anyone. And she wouldn't let another woman be a slave here, either.

She looked straight into Ciara's brown eyes. "You know where Lomdalen is?"

Ciara frowned. "Aye. North."

Ella nodded. "Perfect. Feel like getting out of here?"

FOUR

The next day came and it was supposed to be Channing's bail hearing. He'd had a meeting with Giana, his lawyer, but she'd told him that with so much unrest—thefts, assaults, murders—the jails and courts were full, and his hearing might get postponed.

The day came and went. Then another. The holding cell he'd been in with another thirty people was getting heated. Three fights broke out, one of which ended with an unconscious man being carried out of the cell on a stretcher. Channing was grimy, exhausted from sleeping while sitting on the bench in ten-minute increments, and going mad with worry thinking of what Ella must be going through.

They'd been brought food only once a day. It seemed the global food shortage had reached the police station, too. Hungry, exhausted, on-edge offenders—some of whom were clearly drug addicts going through withdrawal—were not great neighbors. His cellmates were all dressed differently. Some were clearly homeless. Others were just regular folks.

He was the only one in a business suit, the flickering overhead light reflecting from the tips of his shiny black shoes.

He was the only one with a penthouse on top of the Infinity Tower in downtown Boston.

The worst thing about sitting in jail wasn't the bad conditions, the hunger, or the lack of sleep. It was his complete helplessness to do anything to find Ella.

On the third day, they brought in yet more men. There weren't enough places to sit, so some sat on the floor. Channing gave his spot on the bench to an older man, then went to the bars and stared at the hallway with its sickly chipping paint, willing for that door to open and for Ricardo to come and get him out of here and take him to the golden spindle.

Or Giana.

Or even his goddamned Mafia boss grandfather, Leo Esposito.

Anyone, really. As long as he could go straight to the golden spindle.

On the fourth day, the door opened and Ricardo marched in with the blissful call "Hakonson!" The detective's keys rattled as he opened the cell door. "You're needed for an investigation."

Channing dared not hope. Ricardo was purposefully not looking at him, concentrating on the task at hand: cuffing Channing's hands behind his back.

Channing let him do that, waiting for the right moment to ask.

Then Ricardo led him through the police station and into his car. He let Channing get into the back, and Channing already could smell freedom. As they drove away, Channing watched the damned building disappear into the distance. "So? Are we going to the port?"

Ricardo threw a sharp scowl at Channing in the rearview mirror. "Yes."

Channing's stomach flipped. "What took you so long? Who knows where the hell she is now."

Ricardo's nostrils flared, his eyes on the snowed-in road ahead. "The captain wasn't thrilled to let the prime suspect go and help at the crime scene. You could tamper with the evidence. You could escape…"

If all went well, that would be exactly what Channing would do. Ricardo would be in trouble. So Ricardo was risking his career on the chance of helping Ella, even though he didn't completely believe Channing.

"You love her," Channing said. Not a question, a statement.

Ricardo didn't look at him, but his reflection blinked, his mouth straightening. "Yeah."

There it was, the deepest confession a man could make to another. He loved Channing's woman. In any other circumstance, Channing would act differently. Would perhaps warn him off.

But now, strangely, against all odds, they were allies. Rivals united by a common goal, to make sure the woman they both loved was all right.

With eyes straight ahead, Ricardo added, "But she'll never see me that way."

Channing nodded. No more words needed to be said between them. They both knew what this meant.

Ricardo cleared his throat. "Georgina and Munchie are there. I called them. Your time machine is in police custody. XXX It hasn't even been studied yet. There are only a couple of guys guarding it. We don't have the resources with so much going on with this damned cold weather and the food shortage. It seems like people are going more and more insane with every day that passes."

Channing frowned as he looked out the window, automatically watching for any sign of the wolves that had been coming into the city, the wolves that had been following him, protecting him. He didn't see any now. But there were more broken windows, he realized—no one had even bothered to board them up. The snow was piling up, and clearly there weren't enough snowplows to clear it as the roads and sidewalks had turned into snowdrifts. Here and there, fires burned in the alleys between buildings, dark silhouettes of people huddling over them.

"Honestly, I'm not even sure anyone cares about you," Ricardo added. "Maybe that's why it was possible to get you out of jail for a bit. Who cares about another criminal if there are hundreds of new ones every day? Everything is turning upside down. No one really gives a shit who's a real criminal when their brother could be the one killing their wife and children for scraps of food."

Ragnarök...

Brothers killing brothers... The age of the sword. The age of the ax. The age of the wolves...

According to the völva who'd come to his father's hall, he was at fault for all of this... Guilt stung him like a hornet. Channing leaned forward in the car. "Is your family all right?"

Ricardo glanced sharply at him, as though to check if he was for real. "Um. Yeah. Not that it should concern you... We're getting by."

"Good."

"I got my mom and sister out of the city to my uncle's farm in North Carolina. It's safer there, and he has a bit of food stored."

Channing nodded. "Smart. I'd have done the same thing."

Ricardo didn't reply, and the two rode in something that felt like an odd, almost comfortable silence until they reached the port.

It was still operating as it had to accept shipments of food, medicine, and materials into the city and into the country. The police were everywhere, though. Ricardo checked with one of the cops at the front of the gates and they drove through. The cranes by the water moved loading and unloading crates from the vehicles.

Channing saw some people in police uniforms rummaging in the warehouses and taking out the crates with food. Ricardo noticed them as well, his face in the mirror going blank. "The world is coming to an end."

Channing shook his head. "It's fine. Someone should eat. It's worse if the food just goes to waste when the whole world is starving."

Ricardo watched his colleagues pass by through the window, then returned his gaze to the road.

They parked by building M05 and Ricardo got out, then opened the door for Channing. It was awkward to get out while he was still in handcuffs. There were two more cars in the snowed-in and clearly uncleaned parking lot. Georgina and Munchie climbed out of one of the vehicles.

His stomach squeezed in joy at seeing the two people who had made his time in this century close to tolerable.

Dr. Georgina Brandon, a brilliant MIT physicist, was a short, thin Black woman in her early thirties. She walked briskly towards Channing, a huge smile on her face. Channing had never seen more than a chuckle from her in the past and now wondered if, just like he had found Ella at the end of the world, she had found the love of the man she'd worked with for six years while creating the time machine.

The man in question, Dr. Miles Mochizuki, a tall Japanese American man, walked by her side, half turned to her like a protective question mark. Channing liked them together. In an odd way, they were perfect. As a team and as a couple.

Georgina hugged Channing, while Munchie awkwardly clapped him on the shoulder. As Munchie devoured dried mango strips from a small pack one by one, Georgina looked Channing up and down, then looked at Ricardo.

"Do you know what we're going to do, Detective Sanchez?"

Ricardo nodded. "Yeah. You're going to"—he made air quotes—"send him back in time."

The three of them exchanged a look. "Yeah," said Munchie and grinned, also putting air quotes around the word.

They headed to building M05, and when Ricardo opened the door, the two cops who were warming their hands over a portable heater looked up at them.

"Hey, guys," said Ricardo, confidently striding towards them. "The judge has allowed these witnesses access to the crime scene to provide evidence that may help locate Detective O'Connor."

The cops exchanged a look. "If you say so, Detective."

Their expressions of complete indifference astounded Channing for a moment. They looked more interested in warming themselves than in ensuring Ricardo had the proper permission. Ricardo seemed to share Channing's surprise but led everyone to the entrance into the secret basement, which was wide open. They bypassed the yellow security tape and descended the stairs.

The basement was clean now. No cocaine. No blood. No dead bodies.

Only bullet holes.

"Move fast," said Ricardo, and Georgina and Munchie hurried to the control pad.

While they pushed the buttons and turned the gauges, Ricardo undid Channing's handcuffs, and he massaged his wrists.

"Come on..." Georgina mumbled as her fingers flew over

the keys.

Munchie went to the reactor and opened a little door, which revealed a small keypad with glowing green keys. Still chewing, he bent and looked at the screen. "The engine is working." He closed the door. "Let me check the time machine."

Georgina kept typing and pressing on the switches. "Okay."

Munchie looked over the spindle. "It must be the bullet damage. The integrity of the form is compromised. The delicate balance of the runes and the measurements doesn't work." He fingered the bullet hole. "But the bullet has been removed, probably by your forensics team."

"So what do you suggest?" asked Ricardo.

Munchie shined his cell phone's flashlight into the hole. "We have to repair the damage."

"How long will it take?" asked Ricardo. "We don't have all day."

"It won't take all day." Munchie straightened up, took out a small pack of peanuts, and sent a handful into his mouth. "Lucky for you, we do have a kit."

He went to a shelf against the wall, retrieved a small mold, and put it on the concrete floor.

"This should be enough to cover the hole."

He put on protective clothes, a face visor, and thick gloves. Then he took a gas torch from the same shelf and fired it up. A straight orange-blue flame licked the gold. Soon it began glowing and became liquid. He switched off the gas torch. Carefully, with tongs, Munchie picked up the mold and carried it towards the spindle. Slowly, he poured the liquid gold into the hole and used some sort of material to cover the hole so that the metal didn't flow back out.

"Now we wait," said Munchie, removing his gloves.

"How long?" asked Channing.

"Gold solidifies in two to three hours."

Ricardo glared at him. "We don't have two to three hours."

"It might not take so long for the machine to work."

It didn't.

Everything went surprisingly quickly. Only a couple of minutes later, the spindle began spinning, and the golden threads formed and moved around it. But when they passed through it, the area of the bullet hole was like a spot of nothingness.

"Ready to go, boss!" yelled Munchie.

Channing looked at the spindle with suspicion. "Are you sure?"

"It's best you go now." Munchie looked up at the entrance to the basement where the two cops had appeared, their faces worried.

"This was not on the warrant!" yelled one of them.

"Go!" yelled Ricardo.

The cops' feet pounded against the metal stairs as they descended. "Did you put it to the right date and place?" yelled Channing.

"Yes! It may not work perfectly..." Georgina turned a gauge all the way and held it. "But you won't have a better chance!"

With his stomach dropping, Channing reached his hand to the crackling, moving, dancing threads of golden light. He remembered the last time he'd done that—the ninth century, when an old lady with icy-blue eyes had held out a spindle to him, and he'd known it was the only way to save his family.

Now he was doing this again, to save the woman he loved. And as his hand touched the cold, smooth surface of the spindle, it stopped spinning. Everything stopped moving. And like last time, axes cut him into pieces as darkness swallowed him in complete oblivion.

FIVE

The guard outside Ella's door was arguing with someone. His deep voice boomed over another male voice, throwing out insults like "You maggot eater" and "You ant's penis head" and "You pig's arsehole."

When Ciara's voice joined the men's, Ella stood up from her pile of straw, listening. Ciara tried to reason with them, saying all she needed was to pass by them and take some food into the shed.

"No, I will fuck Ciara the slave," said one of the male voices.

"You do not deserve to fuck the slave with your maggot's penis. You did not go with King Harald on the last raid in the Baltic lands. I was there and won him all his silver and new slaves."

"Keep your mouth shut..."

On and on they argued, their pissing contest in some ways completely ridiculous, Ella thought, but on the other hand, nothing she hadn't heard before. Only the insults were more interesting and the threats more real, with the axes and swords no doubt hanging right on the belts of both warriors.

Ella peered through a slit in the wall. Outside, the air was gray and misty in the dusk. Here and there, torches were lit along the dirt-packed streets. Dark smoke rose from the smoke holes into the milky sky over the roofs. The village was quiet, save for the two guards, with most people back in their homesteads for their evening meal.

Probably talking about sheep or cows or fish or the events of their day.

Not whether they'd spent it digging a hole under the wall with their bare hands, scraping their fingernails bloody.

Or whether they'd dreamed about their stepmother's shepherd's pie and their brother's singing and dancing to "Thriller" by Michael Jackson. Or their dad's steely, always suspicious gaze suddenly warming up when he looked at them.

All of that she could still have if she just escaped and found the way back home.

Ciara knew the way. Harald knew it, too.

Channing would have known it, but Channing wasn't here.

But his mother in Lomdalen was. That was where Ella needed to go.

"Hey, you two!" Ella shouted. "How about having a woman from the future?"

It was suddenly so quiet, she could hear the chirping of the crickets.

"Yeah..." She frantically looked around for something to help her fight them. "Not even King Harald himself had me. One of you could be the first."

The table. That was the only thing she could use to her advantage. She had to try again.

She put her hands on the corner and pushed practically at a forty-five-degree angle, digging her shoes into the floor. Perhaps it was the desperation that gave her strength because somehow, it moved. Like a plow, it loosened the packed dirt of the floor. Swallowing her groans, she kept pushing it through the shed.

"He never said she was his," rationalized one of the guards.

"No, he did not. But he does keep one of us on guard. So he does not want anyone else to touch her."

"Or he does not want her to get away," said the first one.

"Please, dinna hurt her..." Ciara said.

While the table was moving, Ella hoped they were idiots enough to not worry about angering King Harald and that they'd be tempted enough by her to just barge in. The table was still breaking through the dirt beneath with its forward leg as she pushed it with her whole body.

"She's a captive," said another one. "King Harald will soon make her a slave. We can hurt her if she's a slave. A slave is nothing."

You ants' penises, thought Ella.

"A slave is not nothing!" she grunted, the sinews of her neck hurting. "I am a human being. Ciara is a human being. And I'm not sure if I can say the same about you. She doesn't want you. But I do."

There was silence again outside.

"You want one of us?" said one of the guards.

"Yes." The table had finally slid right next to the door. It wasn't perfect and it wasn't the best position, but there it was, her best chance for freedom. "Maybe both."

She climbed on top of the table and moved close to the edge to be able to act fast. She plastered herself against the wall.

"I said, you can take me and fuck me, the woman from the future that even King Harald wouldn't touch."

More silence came from outside as the two men were probably thinking about it. "You know," said one of them, "the king never forbade anyone from touching her..."

The door flew open and banged against the wall. The moment the first giant stepped into the shed, Ella stomped him in the head. He groaned, swayed, then turned to her, a grimace of astonishment on his face. Using his momentary disorientation, she grabbed the sword from the sheath on his back. As she pulled it up, her arms sank with the weight of it. With a grunt, she raised it hilt first and smashed the guard's temple. The guy gave out a sharp exhale as his eyes rolled back and he fell on the floor in a large heap.

The second guard, who stood three or four steps away from the door, watched the scene with his jaw hanging, looking at his unmoving friend as if he were staring at a glittery unicorn with a rainbow horn. Ciara picked up a piece of firewood from the pile by the shed and hit him in the back of the head.

A dull thud sounded, but he didn't fall. His eyes bulged, and he bared his teeth in a mask of rage as he turned to Ciara. He sent the piece of firewood flying with a single swipe of his hand. Then he grabbed Ciara by the throat and lifted her up with one arm. Ciara swung her arms and legs, her eyes bulging, face reddening.

Silently, Ella jumped down from the table and walked out of the shed.

She raised the sword with both hands, a small part of her distantly marveling at how great it felt to hold a weapon like this, surprised at how strong and graceful the sword made her feel. Holding a gun was different. Powerful, yes, but not like this. It was as though the sword had energy around it and it gave it to her.

As though she'd been born to hold a sword.

She pressed the tip of the blade into the back of the Viking's neck. "Let go."

He relaxed his fingers, and Ciara fell to the ground like a sack of rocks, coughing and gasping for breath.

Slowly, the guard turned, his eyes hard as steel. "You will not escape."

"We'll see about that. Get in." She nodded towards the shed.

The Viking's jaw worked under his beard, his chest rising and falling faster. Slowly, without taking his eyes off her, he walked into the shed and stepped over his fallen friend. Ella closed the door and lowered the wooden bolt. Right away, the guard started banging against the door. "Escape! Escape!"

Then Ella heard the unmistakable sound of an ax cutting into the wood.

"Escape!" he bellowed again.

Still coughing and holding her neck, Ciara got up. "Over there, Ella." She pointed towards the fjord. "Run! Take a boat, 'tis the best chance ye have."

Ella nodded and ran, Ciara behind her. The wood in the shed cracked with every stroke of the guard's ax as he kept bellowing about the escape. As Ella ran, men and women appeared from the houses, faces alert. Ella's feet pounded against dry, packed dirt as she ran down the slope, gaining speed.

Behind her, somewhere in the distance, male voices yelled, and she knew they must be at her heels. Then Ella and Ciara ran through an open gate and they were on the shore of the fjord. Gravel rustled and rolled under Ella's shoes. Her chest started to hurt as she gulped for air.

At least a dozen small boats were harbored on the beach, and a large Viking ship was docked half a mile along the shoreline. Ella and Ciara ran towards the last boat. Ciara untied it, helped Ella to get in, and pushed it off.

"Row!" Ciara yelled.

"Get in," Ella replied.

"Right away. Ye start, I'll untie the other boats and follow ye. Go on, lass!"

Ella rowed. She had never rowed a boat before, but she used a rowing machine in her gym sometimes. So she let her body do what felt right. Miraculously, it worked, and she moved farther and farther away from the coast.

The voices were growing nearer, and many more male voices than Ella had previously heard. Ciara was untying the other boats, throwing their oars into the fjord and pushing them off into the water. Soon, the coast receded into the distance, and a line of empty boats followed Ella.

When the crowd spilled onto the beach from the village, Ella pressed on, moving her oars as fast as she could, her shoulders burning. King Harald was screaming, pointing his hand at her, then at Ciara.

Why don't you run, Ciara? Run!

But Ciara didn't. She didn't even look at the Vikings. She watched Ella. *Be free...* Ella thought she mouthed.

An icy cold shiver ran through Ella as a dark sense of premonition pressed on her like an invisible hand.

Before she could stop rowing and do something...anything... Harald towered over Ciara. His eyes were on Ella as he grabbed Ciara's hair, pulled her head back, and slit her throat. Blood flowed down her body like wine from a broken bottle, and she collapsed on the ground and didn't move. Shock froze Ella.

A Pictish slave girl had given her life so that Ella could be free.

What an idiot Ella was. She should have insisted Ciara go with her. She should have dragged her into the boat.

It should have been Ciara escaping.

Instead, she had given Ella the most valuable gift of all, especially to a slave—freedom.

A dozen or so people were now in the water swimming, chasing the oars and the boats. A line of men stood along the shore, nocking arrows onto bowstrings. Someone cried, "Aim...shoot!"

Arrows swooshed past her and hit the water around Ella like heavy raindrops.

As one of the arrows struck the oar one inch away from her thumb, she shook off her stupor.

She had to move. She had to run. She couldn't allow Ciara's sacrifice to go to waste.

She rowed. Adrenaline hit her system like caffeine on steroids, and she pumped her arms up and down, pushing the boat away from the coast. One volley of arrows flew, then another one. A fourth and a fifth...

She lost count.

She'd been lucky, as though an invisible shield around her deflected the arrows...

Until it didn't.

Fire shot through her left shoulder as an unstoppable force yanked her backwards and she fell to the bottom of the boat. As she pushed herself up with her right arm, she yelped at the sight of an arrow piercing the soft tissues of her shoulder.

The left oar was floating in the water, behind the boat, too far away to catch.

Blood flowered around the arrow, bright against the grayish white of her dress shirt. Pain tore through her shoulder like claws, and, unable to stop herself, she screamed.

They cheered on the coast, and arrows kept striking the water around her. One of them hit the boat next to her foot.

Blood streamed from her wound faster. She needed to do something to stop it, but first she needed to reach safety. Death was there again, in the air around her, in that fjord, all too familiar by now. She couldn't row with just one oar. Sooner or later, they'd catch up with her.

Helpless and blind from pain, she watched Harald's village drift into the distance, his tall figure standing still on the shore, his gaze firmly on her. Soon arrows couldn't reach her anymore and, after some futile attempts, stopped falling.

Silence fell on the fjord, disturbed only by water splashing against the sides of the boat and her heart thumping in her ears, slow and deafening.

Every breath brought bursts of pain. After a while, when the village was barely visible, she looked down at her wound. She was losing blood—her whole sleeve and the left half of her shirt was soaked crimson. A puddle of blood formed at the bottom of the boat. Adrenaline left her body, and sleepiness enveloped her.

When she couldn't see the village anymore, she let out a large sigh. She knew that she shouldn't remove the arrow until she had proper medical help and the means to stop the blood. She tried to break the shaft, but the movement sank her into a world of agony, and she had to stop. She didn't have the strength in her body to break the wood, especially at this angle.

She needed help, and soon, or she'd die from blood loss or infection. Slowly, she lay on her side on the bottom of the boat and almost lost consciousness from pain. She started shivering —from cold, from shock, and from physical exhaustion. She was afraid to close her eyes and fall asleep because maybe she'd never open them again.

But the soft rocking of the boat and rhythmic splashing of the water against the wood did their job, and soon darkness took her.

SIX

He opened his eyes, while pain was still crushing his bones and his muscles.

The sky was milky gray overhead, and the crowns of trees around him were touched by yellow and orange. Wind rustled leaves and brought faint voices from the distance. It smelled lush, like wet earth and mushrooms, like rotten leaves, and like the woods. And there was a barely distinguishable scent of smoked fish in the air.

No snow.

He sat up and looked around.

A rune stone stood a foot away, light gray, with dark speckles of sand and two rows of Norse runes in the middle of an intricate pattern of the long, interwoven bodies of wolves and dragons.

Wolves and dragons.

Ragnarök...

Ella...

He stood up, his head still empty. This looked good. The

time machine might have worked. He was definitely in Norway, but what year?

He hurried down the hill towards the voices, and as he stepped onto a foot-worn path, the view of a fjord in between mountains made his heart squeeze. Down the path was a village with thatched roofs, longhouses with no windows, and smoke coming out of holes in roofs. Men were wearing tunics and baggy trousers. Women were in apron dresses and had long braids.

A Viking ship was docked by the shore in the distance.

He was in the Viking Age!

Home, he knew. He was home.

He allowed the shock of this to settle in. Fourteen years he'd craved to breathe in this air, to see the sight of these houses and the fjord, to hear this silence. Fourteen years, he'd wanted to be away from the skyscrapers and the crowds, from mobile phones and the scent of gasoline and the constant wail of sirens.

And now he was. It had worked. He'd made it happen. Years of research, two brilliant scientific minds at work, billions invested.

He'd bent the world to his own will.

He'd defied destiny.

As he ran down the path, an icy gust of air stole his breath. Something grayish brown flashed in his peripheral vision, and when he looked between the trees, he saw wolves.

No. Surely, just a coincidence.

He was still in his suit and his dress shirt, his Italian shoes were already covered in mud, and he was freezing cold. How odd it was, to be a modern-day man in the brutal world of the north.

He continued down the slope towards the village, his shoes slipping in the rocky mud of the path.

Was she here? Somewhere in this century, in this country? Was she even alive?

He'd find her and send her back.

The clean air stabbed his lungs like icicles, making his chest burn. The mountaintops high above were white and their cliffs granite gray.

He could feel the presence of the gods here, someone invisible and powerful watching him.

If he was the reason for Ragnarök, they would be watching him for sure.

It would be the end of most of them.

A raven croaked somewhere above... Was it Odin's sign that he was observing Channing even now? The wolves that tracked him were no doubt the descendants of Fenrir, Loki's son.

And those leaden, storm-bearing clouds that hung between the mountains like an iron curtain, did they carry lightning and thunder in them? Would Thor try to strike him with Mjölnir?

A rooster crowed somewhere down the path. Once. Twice. Was it a regular rooster, or one of the roosters that signaled the coming of Ragnarök?

He saw someone coming up the path in the distance and skidded to a halt. His hand reached to the empty space where he'd normally find his sword... He had no sword, no ax, and not even a wooden club. In the twenty-first century, he'd gotten complacent, gotten used to the relative safety of the civilized world. Though he'd kept practicing with his sword to keep himself in shape and to prepare himself for his return to the Viking Age.

He turned left and hid behind a large pine that grew on the side of the path, then peered from behind the tree. The man coming up the path had an ax on his belt and a basket for foraging. He squinted as an icy wind blew right into his face, throwing his long gray hair back and revealing a wrinkled, weathered face.

Had Channing had silver, he could have traded for that ax, even though it was for woodcutting. He needed to know where he was and how far from Lomdalen. If the old man decided to attack him, Channing bet he could protect himself even without a weapon. But first, he'd try to make sure he didn't have to.

He stepped from behind the tree, raising his arms in the gesture of peace. The man stopped, silent, his hand casually resting on the head of the ax hanging by the belt ring. He had just one eye, the other one was covered with a brown leather eye patch. The man looked Channing up and down slowly, the single gray eye lightening with curiosity. Odd, Channing thought, wouldn't a regular man be afraid of someone dressed in a completely different way?

"Where am I?" asked Channing, the words spoken in Old Norse, pleasant and easy on his tongue.

"You are where you are supposed to be, no?"

Channing blinked and let his arms drop to his sides. A strange reply, but not an aggressive one. "I need to go to Lomdalen. Do you know where it is?"

The man nodded slowly, his eye moving to the bushes and undergrowth where, between the trees, brown and gray fur flashed and wolves waited with their heads low and their shoulders rounded, panting like dogs, staring at them.

"North and west," the man said without looking at him, a thoughtful expression on his face. Then he raised his face to the sky where a dozen ravens circled, croaking, above their heads. He raised his left hand in a straight line and pointed into the woods growing on the slope of the mountain. "Go north through the woods until you reach the next fjord. Then follow it west."

Uneasiness scratched at the pit of Channing's stomach. "Thanks. I don't suppose you're interested in trading for clothes?"

He tugged at his suit jacket, opening it up. This was the only thing he could trade, and although it was a highly impractical garment in the Viking Age, the rare fabric might interest a rich merchant, and he might have some old clothes and an ax—that would be all Channing would gladly agree to. He had many challenges before him, and having no weapon and being dressed like a complete outsider were among them.

In this age, outsiders were dangerous.

The single eye looked him over. "A long winter is at our doorstep and all folk are thinking about are furs. You would be better off trading a fox, or even better"—he glanced at the wolves again—"one of those."

A low growl came from the woods, and Channing turned his head to look at the wolves. One of them stared straight at the old man, his nose wrinkled, teeth bared, his head low.

"The damned wolves..." he muttered, but when he looked at the man again, the path before him was empty.

With his stomach sinking, he looked around. "Hey! Where did you go?"

Damn it, he didn't even know the man's name.

The ravens kept croaking over his head, circling, calling. He considered going to the village, but he knew the man was right—no one would consider trading for his clothes, not when the biggest threat to people living in the north was coming. Winter. He could of course ask for charity, beg people to spare things for him, or find work in the village.

Just as he was about to continue down the path, a sound came from somewhere to his right, in the woods. A distressed yell... A high-pitched horse's neigh... It came from the north, exactly where the man had said he was supposed to be going.

He threw a last glance at the small village. He could always return there, but if someone needed his help, he had to help them.

He turned away from the path and jogged right between the bushes, into the thick pine forest, up the hill. His shoes sank into the carpet of wet, soft pine needles. It was uneven and inconvenient, and it took his strength and attention to avoid an odd tree root, to jump over a fallen tree, to avoid the impenetrable undergrowth. And to keep himself from falling.

Damn it. For fourteen years, he'd jogged on asphalt. Straight and hard. He wasn't used to running in nature anymore.

He kept going, feeling the wound from Eirik's sword in one shoulder aching, and the wound from Ragnar's ax in the other. The pine woods grew darker and darker, and the cries and yells grew louder the deeper into the forest he ran.

He smelled it before he saw them. The pungent odor of blood and excrement.

People fought. Between the pines, one blue and one white tunic flashed as two men came at each other with swords. Around them, men lay dead on the ground, axes and swords sticking out from their corpses. Channing swallowed a painful knot. A long time ago, when he had still been a Viking, the sight of the dead had been terrible but not unusual.

Now, a chill ran down his spine.

What had the twenty-first century done to him?

The sound of one sword clashing against another caught his attention. "I killed the deer!" yelled one of the men into another man's face.

"My arrow struck its heart!" cried his opponent.

Ten feet away, a beautiful stag lay staring at Channing with unseeing eyes, its antlers like the branches of Yggdrasil, big and gorgeous.

"You have always been jealous of me!" The first man hammered down his sword on the other, grunting out one word with each strike. "I am Father's favorite!"

"Not anymore," roared the second one. He raised his sword as though he was about to strike down, but as his brother lifted his blade to block, the second man swung his sword from the side in an arcing blow, slicing open the first man's stomach.

The dying man grunted, his mouth open in surprise. His gaze locked on Channing's as he fell and didn't move.

His brother turned around, bloody sword in his hand. As he walked towards Channing, blood dripping from his sword, muscles bulged from under his dark-red tunic, threat written all over his tattooed face. And there it was again, that wildness, that desperation.

Brothers kill brothers... The sword age... The ax age.

He didn't ask who Channing was or what he was doing here. There was nothing in those eyes but mad bloodlust. As the man started running, his sword high above his head, wind threw the first snow into their faces, hard flakes stinging Channing like angry bees. The sky darkened above them, sinking the world into dusk.

Channing backed away from the man. He spotted a corpse a few steps to his right, with an ax sticking out of its chest. He sprinted towards the corpse, the angry brother running after him, screaming something unintelligible.

Making sure he was facing his pursuer, Channing grasped the ax and tried to pull it out, but it wouldn't give. He pulled, stepping on the corpse with one leg and pushing against it to give him more strength, silently begging the dead man to forgive him for treating him with no respect.

The tattooed man raised his sword and slashed.

But the blade never reached Channing. His loyal stalkers, the wolves, jumped on his enemy in a flying wave of fur and teeth and claws. The growling, barking, whimpering horde of wolves swallowed the man, whose scream became a wet gurgle and then died.

Then they backed away, some of their snouts bloodied, and sniffled around him, circling, their scratchy fur brushing against his hands.

And then, they were gone, leaving him standing in the midst of a howling wind and falling snow that started covering dead bodies and melting in the pools of blood.

Channing stood, in the place where he'd wanted to be for fourteen years.

Just him and the growing snowstorm and the dead bodies.

Ragnarök had found him and delivered to him what he'd wanted—weapons, clothes, and loot.

Everything to survive back here and, possibly, to bring about the end of the world.

SEVEN

"What do you guys want?" Channing asked the wolves.

The wolves only turned their ears towards him.

It was the day after the slaughter Channing had encountered and apparently that was all it had taken for him to start talking to the wolves.

One of them was big...giant even, as tall as a deer. He must be the alpha of the pack. Black fur covered his body. His eyes were milky and glowed like two silver moons.

His teeth—long, sharp fangs—could not be completely hidden when he closed his jaws. They protruded from under his black lip, making him look like a monster. He usually held back from getting too close to Channing and was now lying on the ground a little way away, his head resting on his paws.

Channing pushed a burning log deeper into the flames of his campfire. "Are you Fenrir?" he asked the wolf.

The giant raised his head and turned his ears towards Channing.

Channing opened the lid of the field pot and looked inside

at the boiling water. "A giant wolf that would defeat Odin at Ragnarök. Thor would kill him but die later from the wounds inflicted by Fenrir." He stirred the water and added dried, salted meat into his soup. He looked at the big wolf, who locked his eyes with him. "You're Ragnarök itself, aren't you?"

The wolf rose to sit without taking his eyes off Channing.

"Can we forget all this?" he asked. "You guys leave me alone. Go in the woods, hunt rabbits. Let me be."

The wolf lowered his head.

"Look. No one wants the world to end. And you don't want to die in battle, do you?"

Channing stirred the soup, then added a few handfuls of oats he'd looted from one of the dead men's sacks.

He'd found a lot of useful things after the two brothers killed each other. Most important of all, proper Viking clothes. He was ashamed he'd had to disrespect the dead by stealing the clothes off their still-warm bodies, but it was about survival. He'd taken off the tunics, the pants, the cloaks, and the shoes. He'd had to mix and match as some clothes had been cut through with swords and axes.

But the storm had been picking up and he'd had to hurry. Most of all, he needed to make some sort of a shelter. He used the ax to cut the long sticks and build the frame of a shelter in the form of a teepee. Then he cut long pine branches and put them on top of the frame, which served as insulation and protected him from the snow.

It was a rough job, and it was poorly constructed given he'd done it in half an hour. He'd been shielded from the worst of the snow by the pine trees. But by the time he'd finished the shelter, the storm was too strong to stay outside. Channing had stripped fur cloaks from the bodies and taken them into his shelter along with any pouches containing food. Inside, it was barely high enough for him to sit up straight, and his shoulders touched both the trunk of the tree he'd used for the shelter and the pine branches covering the sticks.

He'd lain two fur cloaks over the snowy ground and used two more as blankets. Shivering, he lay in the darkness, listening to the wailing of the wind and the soft, endless clicks of snowflakes, carried by the strong wind, hitting the roof of his shelter.

When he was warm enough, he slept.

The next morning, the storm had stopped. Perhaps two inches of snow had fallen. He'd had a quick breakfast of dried fish. Then he looked through the now-frozen dead bodies and found more useful stuff. A fire steel for starting fires meant the difference between life and death in the outdoors. He found a knife that he could use for dressing fish and game and also for eating. The ax was useful, and he took the best sword he found.

He'd grabbed all the food he could find and looked with regret at the beautiful stag that had been hunted by the brothers yesterday. This stag would feed him alone for a good week or perhaps even ten days if he was careful. Plus, that gorgeous hide could be used for shoes, for a belt, as well as to repair weapons and make shelters. But he couldn't waste time and energy dressing the frozen carcass.

He'd found a good traveling backpack and added two more long wolf cloaks. They would be useful for sleeping and keeping himself warm. He already had one on his shoulders. He took the invaluable cast-iron field pot as well as a ladle and a small bowl.

He also took all the silver he found. Silver could buy him passage, a warm place to spend the night, and perhaps even military protection. Any of that could mean being able to find Ella faster.

When he'd had the backpack on his shoulders, the ax and the sword on his belt, and a walking stick in his hand, he'd looked around the snowed-in battlefield. Ravens had started circling in the sky above the dead, waiting for Channing to leave so that they could have their feast. With wolves watching his every move, Channing had walked.

North and west, the old man had said.

North and west Channing went, following one thought.

Ella.

The pack of wolves tailed him like a shadow. He'd made his first stop when he'd found a good place for a rest. A spot where the ground was clear of snow, there were enough old, dead trees to find firewood and a spring with clean water was about thirty feet away.

He'd started the fire. Started the soup.

Started talking to the wolves.

The big one still stared at him. There was no consciousness in that stare, Channing knew. No reflection. No understanding. No soul.

"Why am I trying to negotiate with a predator?" Channing murmured as he poured the soup into his bowl. As he slurped the hot liquid that warmed his body from the inside, the wolf he'd decided to call Fenrir licked his jaws. "And yet, this predator follows me like a loyal dog."

Channing made a similar shelter and spent the night there. The next morning, he kept going. North and west. North and west.

Day after day passed. He crossed mountains and woods. On the fourth day, he reached another fjord. On the fifth day, his food came to an end. But it didn't worry him as much as Ella.

That day, a fog settled on the fjord so thick, he could eat it by the spoonful. It was hard to see more than one step ahead.

He got a fire going despite the humidity. As he sat on the ground, listening to the firewood crackle, he dozed off.

"Ulf Hakonson."

His Norse name, not the name he used in modern times. His mother had always called him Channing, the Celtic name that meant wolf, just as his Norse name did.

The voice woke him and he jerked to sit up. A small figure in a dark cloak stood before him... She put the hood down.

His heart dropped down to his feet. Whenever he saw the plum-colored, wrinkled cheeks, the icy-blue eyes, and the white hair, it meant trouble. Last time, she'd sent him to the twenty-first century.

He jumped to his feet. "Norn," he said.

"You need to wake up and follow the shore to the west. Hurry. She doesn't have long."

Channing blinked. "Who? Ella? What happened?"

The Norn nodded. "Hurry."

Opening his eyes, he frantically looked around. No Norn. Just the trees, the muddy, rocky ground covered with dead leaves. His fire almost completely died down.

The fog had dissipated and lifted up a little.

West, she'd said. Channing jumped to his feet, stuffed his fur cloak into his backpack, and extinguished the fire.

He ran down the shore of the fjord, heading west.

She didn't have long.

ELLA WAS BURNING. Fire licked her flesh, incinerating her, corroding her, making her moan and beg and plead for it to stop.

She didn't know how much time passed as she drifted in the boat. The edges of the mountains moved past her from both sides, gray clouds floating through the endless milky sky.

Everything was blurry, and she was weak, so weak, and there was only that evil fire in her shoulder. That eternal pain.

She'd probably die here. Blood loss was one thing, but now she clearly had a fever. Poor Ciara, she'd died in vain.

And Channing...the man she loved like she loved no one else... She shouldn't have pushed him away like she had. She should have believed him, trusted that he was innocent. She should have used every second to kiss him, to hold him, to just breathe the same air as him.

She should have told Ted and Dad and Gloria how much she loved them every single day. She should have spent more time with Ricardo. With other friends she used to have before she'd pushed everyone away, believing sooner or later they'd leave her.

It was too late now. She'd die somewhere in the middle of the fjord, back in the ninth century. Archeologists might find her skeleton. What would they think about her? Would they wonder if she was a Viking's wife? Maybe they'd see a scratch on her shoulder bone and wonder if she was a warrior woman...

She was probably delirious.

She needed to keep her eyes open, but they were so heavy. Soon, dusk descended on the world. The mountains became black shapes, and the sky was like diluted ink.

The woods were moving closer...she must be approaching the shore. She could distinguish curly crowns of trees, and then the splashing against the sides of the boat grew louder, and it softly thumped into something and stopped.

Where was she? Oh God, if Harald found her, she wouldn't be able to defend herself or even run.

Maybe she was dreaming. Yes, there was pain, but pain could be in her dreams, too, right?

She took a deep breath, preparing herself for the avalanche of pain that she knew would come, then sat up, almost fainting from the agony.

She must have landed in a cloud. Fog hung on the water and on the shore, thick as whipped cream. Obsidian shapes of trees, boulders, and cliffs darkened through the mist. It was quiet, almost unnaturally so. No birdsong, no rustling leaves, no buzzing insects.

Dead quiet.

A chill crawled down her feverish body.

Then a silhouette appeared up the shore through the fog. As a soft breeze blew past her, it cleared her view. It was a female figure in a cloak standing and looking in her direction.

Help...she could ask for help...

Slowly, restraining her groans as pain shot through her in high-voltage bolts, she climbed out of the boat, almost falling into the water. Then, feeling like she was flying, she moved up the hill and towards the figure. The whole world was careening left and right as though she were on a ship in a storm.

Everything blurred, and as she took the next step, her foot betrayed her on an uneven stone. She lost her balance and fell awkwardly on her behind.

Her whole body exploded in blinding pain. She yelled out, then ordered herself to shut up. Screaming in this silence could be a death sentence.

She froze and breathed, riding the pulsating waves of agony. When she could open her eyes again, she pushed against the ground, which was covered with old, dry leaves, and sat up straighter.

The hooded figure stood right in front of her, and Ella blinked, commanding her vision to focus and see who it was.

A sweet old lady, a grandmotherly type, with sharp blue eyes and plump, rosy cheeks. White hair done in a braid crowned her head. She wore a dark cloak, under which an apron dress showed—the surprisingly bright-green color of it hurt Ella's eyes.

"Hello, sweetheart," the woman said. "I am sorry to see you in such distress."

Her voice was melodic, pleasant, an old woman's voice. Something about it was so familiar... Something about her struck a chord of melancholy in Ella's chest and accelerated her heartbeat.

"Um... Can you help me? I need a doctor," Ella said.

The woman leaned closer to her and cupped her face, and Ella's stomach flipped as she looked into the woman's eyes. It seemed as if they had no bottom. There was something eternal and eerie about their icy-blue depths.

"You think you are lost, sweetheart?" the woman asked. "But you are right where you are supposed to be."

"Wha—"

"Destiny brought you here, Ella. Ragnarök is coming, and you have a bigger role in it than you realize."

Her head spun, darkness creeping into her vision. Ragnarök...her role... Pain grasped her in its clawed fist, sucking in the last of her energy.

"Trust, my love..." she heard as though from far, far away.

Then she let scorching darkness take her.

"Ella! Ella!"

Cold...sweet, dear cold was sucking the evil fire away...

"Ella..."

That voice...she knew it. It had sworn loyalty to her once, it had told her he would do anything for her...

"Ella, sweetheart, wake up..."

But it couldn't be. He was far away. In another time. No way to get to her.

As the cold on her forehead shielded her from the fire, she found the strength to open her eyes.

Above her, bloody and tired, and so, so dear, was Channing.

EIGHT

Channing held her in his arms, and she smelled like blood, and a little fishy, like the fjord.

Across time, through enemies and a world that was tumbling to its end, he'd found her. The woman he'd been searching for his whole life and didn't even know he needed. The woman he breathed for, his blood pumped for, his very soul ached for like for a prayer.

"Ella..." he whispered into her tangled hair. "I'm so sorry this happened to you. I'll help you recover, I promise. I'll get you to my mother."

He spoke the usual American English he hoped would comfort her.

He spread a wolf cloak on the mossy ground and carefully laid her down on top of it. The shore was twenty or so feet away down the slope. It was silent, a strange fog hanging along the fjord. It seemed to move away now, although there was no wind.

She looked ashen, no doubt had lost a lot of blood judging

by that caked sleeve and the side of her shirt. She'd stopped losing blood, thank goodness, as far as he could tell, but she was as hot as a furnace. No doubt she had an infection...the most dangerous thing in a time without antibiotics.

He really needed to get her to Lomdalen, to his mother... And back to the twenty-first century as soon as possible. But first, he needed to get the fucking thing out of her body. The wound had almost certainly accumulated plenty of bacteria and may have dirt in it, as well.

She stroked the side of his face with her palm, and the touch was like a soothing balm to him. "Are you even real?"

He smiled, leaning into her touch, and grasped her hand, pressing it tighter to his face, craving every touch, every caress, every moment with her. "I am, Ella. I'm here, right here, with you."

She blinked, the feverish blush on her cheeks bright. He didn't like the dilated pupils, the paleness of her skin, the shivers that ran through her body. Even though he'd found her, and relief relaxed his very core, she was still not out of danger yet—far from it.

She sighed. "How did you even find me?"

"One of the Norns came to me in a dream and told me to go west and find you. That you didn't have much time. She was right."

"Are you serious? What did she look like?"

"Old. White hair. A braid around her head. Blue eyes."

She blinked. "That was the same woman who told me I was where I was supposed to be and that I have a bigger role in Ragnarök than I realize."

"You saw the Norn, too..." he murmured. "And she didn't give you or me the golden spindle. What does all that mean?"

Ella closed her eyes and swallowed. "I don't know. But I don't like these Norns. Most powerful beings in the world my ass... What good does it do when they watch the end of the world unfold and do nothing?"

"That's not true. She led me to you." He looked around. "But the most important thing now is to take care of you."

He had no medicine, no sterile materials, nothing. Ella had thought that stitching his cut in his apartment with his first aid kit was barbaric.

Look at him now. Nothing with him but an ax, the clothes on his back, and the rest of the loot he'd gotten from the dead men.

And he was already panicking.

The damned Viking Age. He'd lived here for eighteen years, and yet fourteen years in the twenty-first century had made him a different man.

A complacent man.

The twenty-first century had made him weak, soft. He'd learned to rely on technology too much. A simple thing like the lack of electricity would set humankind back several centuries. Here, he had to rely on survival skills, combat skills, and physical strength.

First things first, he needed to light a fire, then build a shelter, then take care of Ella's wound as best as he knew how with what he'd been given.

"Wait here, sweetheart," he whispered. "I'll take care of you. I'm right here."

She grabbed on to him like a child, panic crossing her beautiful features. It killed him to see her like that. He wanted to tear the whole world apart to make sure she was all right.

"I'll just get some wood and start the fire, all right? I'm right here."

"Oh." She nodded, clearly trying to get herself together. "Okay."

He kissed her firmly on her forehead and darted away,

quickly identifying dry branches that would catch fire quickly and some dry moss and old grass. He gathered more wood for the fire and peat moss to treat Ella. Soon, flames played in the campfire, illuminating Ella's shiny, feverish eyes. She shivered, huddling into her clothes.

He'd noticed a small waterfall up the hill that fell into the fjord. He gathered water from there into his field pot and put it over the fire to boil.

He had to do the unspeakable. He had to hurt his woman. Channing looked at the small knife he had taken from one of the men.

"This should work." He bit his lip and shoved the small blade right into the fire, making sure the handle was safe from the flames.

"What for?" she asked, her eyes so trusting and big.

Channing's stomach in knots, he ran his fingers through his hair. "You have an infection. I have to stop it."

Her eyes dropped to the blackening knife and her face went blank. "Oh."

"I'm sorry, I have to. I'll break the arrow and pull it out. Thankfully, it looks like a clean shot through your muscle. I have treated wounds like that on the battlefield... But burning the wound is the only way I have to stop the infection."

Ella closed her eyes and nodded. "I bet you're laughing now at how squeamish I was about stitching you."

"I'm not laughing when it comes to your life and your health."

Ella sighed and leaned back. "Do it. I feel it, the infection. The fever...the pain...it can't get much worse than this."

Channing took her hand in his. "We are still a few days from Lomdalen. I can't take the risk of waiting until we reach my mother. But if I do what I can now, you'll have the chance of reaching her. I can't—" His voice broke and he cleared his throat, resuming with more strength than he thought he had. "I can't lose you. Not again."

There was fear in the depths of her feverish eyes. But his brave girl didn't fall apart.

She didn't know what was coming to her. He'd literally burn her flesh while she was completely conscious, no anesthesia, no painkiller, not even alcohol to sink her into oblivion.

"That woman," Ella murmured, "she told me to trust. You trusted me to stitch you up. I'll trust you to do what you need to do. I'm just so glad you're here..."

On an impulse, he leaned down and kissed her, holding on to her as though otherwise she'd slip away from him. Her lips were hot and dry, and she clung to him, one weak hand wrapped around his neck.

He loved her. He'd found her. He'd never let her go...

And yet, he'd have to hurt her. He gently pulled back and pressed his forehead against hers. "I'll get you to Lomdalen, get you well, and find a way to send you back to the twenty-first century where you'll be safe. Are you ready?"

She nodded. "As ready as I'll ever be."

He undid the leather belt on his waist and gave it to her. "Bite this. This is so that you don't bite your tongue off."

Her eyes widened for a moment, then she nodded and took the belt in the hand of her unwounded arm. The water boiled in the small pot. He tore a strip off his tunic, which he'd use to stop the blood once he'd pulled the arrow from her wound.

He placed the strips of fabric into the boiling water—at least that would kill the bacteria—then took the pot off the fire.

"Turn to your side."

She did, with her back to him.

"Bite the belt, Ella. I'm going to break the arrow now."

When she'd put the belt in her mouth, he broke the arrow as cleanly as he could. She whimpered, and he hated himself for hurting her even a little.

"Hold on, sweetheart. I'm going to pull it now."

She nodded. His brave, strong girl.

He exhaled and told himself to hold it together. He'd done this a few times when he fought in the Viking Age, but had never liked doing it. And those were men, his sword-brothers, who were trained and raised, knowing that the way of a warrior was often the way of pain.

This was the love of his life. The woman he'd die for. And he would cut off his own arm sooner than hurt her.

Yet he had to.

Shutting out his guilt and fear, he focused on the task at hand. He told himself this was just like back then, on one of the battlefields, and this was his sword-brother who needed help.

He pulled the arrow in one quick motion. Ella grunted in a long, excruciating shriek of pain, muffled by her biting the belt. The blood started flowing as the wound reopened, and Channing grabbed the still-hot strips of linen and pressed them against her wound.

Then everything was a blur, like a movie that flashed by in fast-forward. Under Ella's screams of agony, he stopped the blood as well as he could. Commanding himself to forget that it was her, he pressed the red-hot blade to one side of her wound, then the other.

The scent of burning flesh reminded him of a barbecue, making bile rise in his stomach.

Her screams tore his soul for an eternity, and then, suddenly, they stopped. He made a dressing for her wound out of peat moss and tied it around her arm. Peat moss, known in the twenty-first century as sphagnum moss, killed the bacteria and cleaned up the blood. His mother and other healers used it to dress wounds.

Then he turned Ella on her back. She shook and whimpered. He gently removed the belt from her mouth—she'd almost bitten through it. Her eyes were wild, dark, as if she were a trapped animal with nowhere to hide and nowhere to run.

She must hate him.

"Come here," he said as he curled over her, pulling her into his embrace.

But even with the little strength she had, she jerked away, as though he was her torturer.

No...

She'd never forgive him for the pain he'd caused her. He'd understand.

He nodded and covered her with the edge of the wolf cloak she was lying on. The pot of water had now cooled down sufficiently to be drinkable and not to burn her, and he brought it closer to her.

"Drink, sweetheart. You lost a lot of blood and you're dehydrated."

She nodded and he helped her by holding her head straight with one hand and the pot of water with the other.

She was falling asleep now, and he cradled her head in his arms, saying blessings and making prayers for health to Freya in his mind.

Only, even though he was now in the time he'd wanted to return to for fourteen years, the words felt foreign and empty. And then, in the dusk, he saw pairs of glowing eyes...

And from the shadows among the trees, the wolves came. Gray, brownish, yellowish fur whitening against the darkness, they approached him, staring at him.

The alpha came closer, holding something in his mouth,

and laid it right in front of Channing, sniffing the air around him.

A hare.

The wolves had found him again, caring for him, protecting him, making sure he was alive.

Making sure he'd bring this world to its end.

NINE

A wet heat... Her body felt heavy and ached and her mind was like a swamp. Something was bothering her...something hurt.

Her shoulder. She opened her eyes, suppressing a groan of pain. In the dim gray daylight, a Viking watched her... Brown hair in a man bun, Viking tattoos, warm brown eyes...

It was her Viking.

Channing, only he wasn't dressed like a billionaire anymore. He looked like a real Viking now. Leather armor over a linen tunic, an ax on his belt, baggy Viking pants, and thick leather half boots with thin soles and laces around the ankles.

"It's all right, sweetheart," he said. "You're safe. I got you."

His voice calmed her down, made her feel safe. Somehow, he'd found her.

He'd cauterized her wound... He'd saved her life.

She looked around. Ah, the dim light was because they were in a cave. A campfire burned three feet away from her, with a small field pot standing next to it and steaming. Water...

Still woozy, she smacked her dry lips, her mouth feeling

like sandpaper, and tensed her core to sit up. Pain shot through her as she moved her wounded arm.

He helped her to sit up and lean against the wall of the cave. He wrapped the sides of the fur cloak around her shoulders. One sleeve of her shirt was ripped off and her wound was bandaged. Something green was stuck between her burn and the bandage, green stains mixing with the brown stains of dry blood. Cold air chilled her skin, and she noticed in the mouth of the cave that thin snow was falling and the ground was powdered with white.

"How long was I out?" she asked, her words slurred and slow.

He leaned down and picked up the field pot. "Two days. Drink this." He handed it to her, and she accepted it, and warmth spilled through her palms as her fingers encircled the pot. "You were in and out of high fever, delusional. You thrashed and moaned in my arms, so hot you could melt *Fimbulwinter*. I thought... I thought this was it."

The liquid in the pot must be broth; it smelled like cooked meat, and her stomach growled. She put the pot against her mouth and drank the meaty liquid. Although it was unseasoned, nothing had ever tasted as good.

"Yum," she said, chewing a small chunk of meat.

"Are you hungry?"

"I think I am."

"That's a good sign."

He reached for something wrapped in leather and tore out a grilled leg. "A hare," he said, handing it to her.

She took it with her good arm and bit into the meat. It was chewy and tasted strong and plain, but it was food. "Mmm. Thanks."

"How's your shoulder?"

"You know...feeling like an arrow pierced it."

"Hurts?"

"Let's just say, Doctor, give me all the pain meds. All of them."

He sighed. "As soon as we get to Lomdalen, we'll find a way to send you back to your time. I promise you."

She nodded. "That would be great. I'm so worried about Dad and Ted and everyone."

He picked up a knife and a piece of wood and started cutting off thin white shavings. "I'm worried about you."

Condensation steamed out of his mouth as he breathed.

She bit into the meat and chewed more. After she swallowed, she said, "What I don't understand is how I ended up here."

"I thought you could tell me that. The spindle was completely out. It took Munchie and Georgina a while to get it to work to send me here."

She slowly shook her head, trying to remember what she had done, what she had thought... "I really have no idea. How did you manage to travel in time?"

"Ricardo arrested me, but your dad and Ted came to visit me, and they pretty much convinced Ricardo to let me go and find you."

"Oh... How are they?"

"They're fine, just worried about you, but they're fine."

"Damn it." Her gut churned, threatening to send back the few bites of meat she'd eaten.

"I'll find the way, Ella," he said firmly as he dragged the knife along the stick. "You won't stay here for much longer. I promise. Not while Ragnarök followed me here."

Her whole face went limp. "What?"

He nodded at the mouth of the cave. "Look. Winter. The damned wolves are following me again, bringing me food, protecting me..."

He stopped cutting and stared at the knife and the wood in his hands.

"What?" she pressed.

"The unrest...it is here, too. Brothers killing brothers... That's how I found the ax, the sword, the clothes, and the rest..."

A chill brushed down her spine like an icy hand.

Channing pressed the knife against the stick and pushed it down slowly. "It's only September," Channing said thoughtfully. "They just gathered the harvest and are hunting and fishing to store meat for the winter. But food will become sparse quickly if people are busy fighting each other and not storing food. We might have the same situation on our hands as we did in Boston."

She leaned her head back against the rocky wall and let it rest there, chewing, thinking. "I just don't understand. How can one person be responsible for the end of the world?"

"The time machine, I think. I used science to manipulate the course of life...the course of history. I think the Norns don't like that."

"But I used your time machine, too. Am I the reason for Ragnarök, too?"

He stopped cutting. Silence hung between them in the cave as they both stared at each other. "No," he said firmly. "There was nothing in the prophecy about you. It's all on me. Although what puzzles me is that when I was eighteen and the völva came to tell King Harald the prophecy, I hadn't built the time machine yet."

"Yes, that a good point."

"Exactly. A lot of it doesn't make much sense, and I have to find a way to resolve this. So once we get you back to the twenty-first century, you can forget all this."

"Forget all this? How can I ever forget you?"

He went so still, she could see the tiny vein on his temple beating, just above his heart-shaped birthmark.

"Are you..." he said, his voice rasping, urgent. "Are you well enough? I want to kiss you, but not unless—"

Suddenly the need to feel his lips on hers, his arms around her, his scent in her nostrils was stronger than any pain, than any worry. "I'm well enough."

She dropped the hare leg on the floor of the cave. He dropped his knife and the wooden stick.

In one movement he was by her side, gently cupping her face with his hands. He planted a kiss on her lips, and she forgot all pain and all worry. As he drank from her mouth, softness enveloped her. His scent was different here; mixed with woodsmoke and animal furs and the crispness of snow, it made her head spin. Tingles rushed through all over, melting her bones. He deepened the kiss, delicious and possessive, and a small tremor ran through her. The tension in her body dissolved, and everything except for him stopped existing around her.

After a while, he pulled away, both of them panting, staring at each other. "Don't stop," she whispered. "I'm fine."

"You have no idea how I want to keep kissing you...but you're not fine, Ella. You never told me, how did this happen? What happened to you when you traveled in time?"

She leaned back against the wall again and picked up the hare leg, brushing it off. "Your dear friend the king found me."

"What?"

She chuckled. "Yeah. Imagine. He was right there when I appeared out of thin air. Got all excited, knew I was a time traveler, locked me up in the shed for days."

"I will kill him."

She decided not to mention the part where Harald wanted

to make her his concubine. She knew Channing would become enraged, and that wouldn't help the situation.

"I escaped. A sweet slave girl helped me." Sadness choked her throat as she remembered how easily Ciara's throat had opened under Harald's knife. "I was in a boat, and they shot arrows after me. One of them hit me…but my boat kept going and they lost me. I don't know how long I was in that boat. Then there was an old woman who told me I have a bigger role to play… And then you came."

He pulled her into a hug, careful not to hurt her shoulder. "I'm so sorry you got hurt," he whispered into her ear. "I promise I won't let anything like that happen to you again."

She clung to him, grateful for his company, for the promise of his protection and care. "Just get me home."

"We'll leave as soon as you feel better. It's just down the fjord."

They spent two more days like that—talking, cuddling. Channing went to set the snares for hares and brought two that he'd dressed and boiled. He worked on making a second oar for the boat, which he had brought closer to their cave and hidden. Ella was regaining her strength, although moving her arm was still incredibly painful.

The cave, even though cold and hard, felt safe. There was something primitive about this, and she wished she wasn't wounded and they could cuddle under those furs naked and warm each other up.

She'd never been in a position where she had completely and totally depended on a man—for everything. Channing fed her, brought her water, kept the fire going, kept watch at night. If he left her here alone, she'd be done.

But she knew he wouldn't.

And with every day that passed, she realized, she wasn't the same as she was in the twenty-first century. The old her wouldn't rely on him.

But surprisingly for her, she trusted him completely.

On the third day, Channing was out for a while and Ella was resting, caught between sleep and daydreaming.

Black against the white light of the day, his big frame appeared in the mouth of the cave. She sat up straight and he came to help her stand. "We must leave now. He found us."

TEN

Channing's heart raced. "Quickly, to the boat."

Dozens of feet murmured against the thin layer of snow, and dogs barked in the distance. Supporting his woman with one hand as they hurried down the rocky slope, Channing glanced back. Up the slope, warriors with axes and swords in their hands sprinted across the uneven ground, zigzagging between the pines.

Someone pointed at them and yelled to the others. Adrenaline hit Channing's system like a burst of fire. He had to save her. He couldn't allow them to get to her.

"Sweetheart, can you run?" he asked, accelerating.

"Yes."

She sprinted, sliding, almost falling down the slippery snow. He hurried along with her, still supporting her with his arm. If she fell, the crust on her wound could reopen and the bleeding would start again.

They were finally on the gravelly beach on the shore of the fjord. He'd hidden the boat behind the cliff that protruded into the water, and their enemies wouldn't be able to see them if they got in.

Something thin and dark swooshed past him, and an arrow hit the ground five steps before him. More arrows followed, raining down on them.

"Odin's cock!" he muttered.

Still hurrying towards the fjord, he looked over his shoulder. Archers stood high up on the slope of the mountain, which contained the cave Channing and Ella had hidden in. There must have been two dozen of them and they had the perfect position to shoot, standing on the rocks of the slope. Other warriors, wielding swords and axes, hurried after them.

He could only pray to the gods for the arrows to miss. One arrow and he or Ella would be finished.

And then, as though the gods laughed at his prayer, he was proven wrong.

His head was still turned to the enemy when he saw an arrow whizzing through the air towards him. He could almost feel the sharp tear of the flesh on his back, the explosive pain, the shock of the impact.

There it was, heading right for him one moment, almost piercing him through...

And then, out of nowhere, Ella pulled him to his right, and away. The arrow barely scratched the side of his sleeve and hit the ground with a soft thump.

She was pale, her eyes milky from exhaustion as she kept moving forward, stumbling, panting. Had she seen the arrow coming, too? Where did she find the strength?

"Not now," she barked.

As another wave of arrows hit the ground around them, he pulled his head into his shoulders instinctively.

"Thanks..." he said, still feeling the chill crawling down his sweaty back like tiny, icy ants.

They were already almost at the fjord. They would just

need to follow a tiny streak of wet gravel around the giant granite cliff, then there it would be, the boat.

Only, a horde of the enemy appeared from behind a hill to their left, including a man who made Channing stop dead in his tracks.

The long red beard hanging in a single oiled braid. The intricate helmet, its dull silver glimmering white as it reflected the thin layer of snow that powdered the ground and the mountain. A rich sword glistened as the man moved his arm, balancing as he hurried down the rocky slope. Unlike most of his warriors, he wore a rich *brynja*—rare, expensive chain mail that only the wealthy could afford.

The expression of a predator was on his face. An expression Channing had welcomed when they had been on the same side. Back then, Channing and his father, Hakon, had fought for him, risking their lives to put him on the throne of the united Norway.

Now that man wanted him dead.

As Channing and Ella kept moving, King Harald yelled something, pointing at them. He was still far away, and they still had time.

Until they didn't. Probably losing her last strength, Ella stumbled, but Channing managed to catch her. Her eyes were rolling back, her face ashen. *To all gods, please don't let her wound be reopened!*

Without a word, he picked her up and allowed himself one last look at his enemy.

Harald was much closer now, and he didn't run. He stood frozen, like a statue, his brows knitted together in one straight line, his eyes wild and wide as though he'd just seen a dead man rise from the grave.

His mouth opened and he roared, pointing his sword at

Channing, "This is him—Ulf Hakonson! Take him! Stop him! Kill him!"

King Harald's men echoed a battle cry and sped up, still yelling as they ran at him, their weapons sharp and glinting, ready to kill.

And not just him.

Her.

Channing turned around and ran towards the cliff rising high above him, but he was slow with Ella in his arms, so much slower than the enemy. If they reached him, he'd need to put her down and fight... And they could take her away from him or hurt her.

Arrows were still striking the ground around him as gravel crunched under his feet, and several arrows scratched and tore his clothes. He was at the farthest corner of the protruding cliff. When he finally turned the corner, the arrows couldn't reach him. The gravelly shore dipped sharply into the water and he had to slow down here. His leather boots quickly took in water.

He kept going. Water splashed loudly behind him, and when he turned, he saw them beyond the cliff, just fifty or so steps away. His lungs burned, his muscles aching and his shoulder wound screaming with pain.

But all his efforts would pay off if he and Ella could escape. There it was, the boat, which he'd carefully turned over on the gravel. It was now covered with a thin layer of snow and partly frozen with ice. Damn it! They were too many and they were too close. He'd have put Ella down, turn the boat over, and drag it to the water.

The closest warriors were ten feet away, panting, arms and legs pumping as they ran through water.

He'd give anything to escape now. He'd even call the wolves... Where were they when he needed them?

Just as he thought that, a distant howl carried through the

air, then another came, closer. Animal growls and woofing sounded nearby. Were they *his* wolves? Relief spread in his gut as he reached the boat and gently put Ella on the gravel. He turned the boat over, and behind him, the growls, the angry yapping were mixed with human grunts of pain and screams. As he dragged the boat towards the water, he could clearly see the wolves coming to his rescue yet again.

Had he somehow called for their help without realizing?

If he was the force of Ragnarök, they were his army, for better or for worse.

He put Ella into the boat and pushed it, congratulating himself for making the second oar—it would save their lives. He jumped into the boat and began rowing, ignoring the tearing pain in his shoulder. Watching the shore disappear into the distance, he could see the pack of wolves fighting his human enemies. King Harald wielded his sword, his red beard flashing.

But even from this distance, Channing could see the angry astonishment on the man's face. As Channing worked the oars, desperately forcing the boat towards Lomdalen, he saw Harald stab one of the wolves. The animal fell, whimpering, and Harald stood, panting and staring after Channing.

They were now too far away to hear anything, but with his crimson sword, Harald pointed straight at Channing, blood dripping into the snow.

ELEVEN

There it was, Dragon's Tongue Mountain, just a thirty-minute hike away from Lomdalen, with its cliff piercing the air like a blade two thousand feet above the fjord—a fact that Channing had learned in the twenty-first century.

The rock stuck out like giant balcony, the place his father had taken him many times to hike and hunt and look at the incredible view, the flat snake of the fjord slithering between the mountains, the endless gray sky. Sitting with his father as a boy, Channing had often wondered what lay beyond the horizon, what else there was in the world besides this.

Sognefjord, on which Lomdalen lay, was the longest fjord in Norway, and since Channing didn't know exactly where he was when he'd found Ella, he'd known Lomdalen could be anywhere down the fjord. It had taken them the whole day and the night to reach it.

Ella had come to her senses an hour or so after they'd escaped. They'd spent the night huddled in the wolf cloaks, keeping warm. It had been the coldest night of his life, but they'd managed to survive. In the morning, he'd kept rowing while he could, but his wound was aching and he wanted to conserve some strength in case Harald found them again. With impenetrable cliffs and mountains on both sides of the fjord, the only way to keep going was by boat. They were both dehydrated because they couldn't drink from the fjord, which contained seawater. They'd eaten the last of the grilled hare, and were now hungry.

Channing turned to Ella and resumed rowing. "We're here, Ella."

"What, really? Here?" The boat shifted as she sat up. "Wow..."

Wow, indeed.

The air smelled like snow, like wet earth and seawater. Which felt wrong at this time of year when the leaves were still green. Snowflakes started falling, tiny and slow, melting on the water. It smelled like that in November, he knew, when winter would take its firm grip. Behind the cliff of the Dragon's Tongue would be Lomdalen.

Home.

He picked up the oars and kept rowing. As if in a dream, he moved too slowly, water dragging the boat down as though an invisible beast didn't want him to arrive. But with every splash of the oars, every push forward, they got closer. After a few minutes, he could already see the fishing boats out in the fjord, then a few trade ships, and finally, there, his father's pride...his dragonship, a beast that needed sixty rowers and could transport a hundred warriors.

The ship he'd made his first raid with, the ship he'd grown from a boy to a man on.

A few more strokes, and there, on a hill by the fjord, appeared Lomdalen.

Single-story, dark wooden longhouses with thatched roofs, white with snow now, no windows and just holes in the roofs to vent smoke out. His father's mead hall up the hill, a majestic building by Viking Age standards. Tall, long, solid, with a big gate, intricate Norse carvings of dragons he couldn't yet see but remembered like it was yesterday. The paths between the houses were paved with wooden planks and in parts with cobblestones, an innovation his mother had suggested.

His mother...with her medicinal herb garden a few steps away from the mead hall. It should still be able to provide her with herbs in September, but had no doubt been knocked out by the early cold snap.

He'd wanted to come back here for so long, and it had always been impossible.

Only, he'd made the impossible possible. He'd created a time machine to save his family from a death in a fire. He'd read about the fire that would kill them in one of the Icelandic sagas still preserved in the twenty-first century and decided he had to return and warn his family.

He'd escaped the police and the Mafia, and he'd crossed time.

Now, he realized, he might be able to save them from the fire, but he might bring a worse death to their doorstep.

"Is this where you grew up?" Ella asked.

He turned to her, and his stomach flipped in something like excitement...pride...

Love.

Not long ago, he'd invaded her home and met her family, where he'd yet again realized how much he missed his.

"Yeah," he said. "This is it." His core burned, contracted with emotion. "Home." He choked the last word out.

To see his father, his mother, his brother, and his sister again...

His eyes connected with Ella's, and she caught him, open, vulnerable. He let her see it, the depth of the yearning that had been driving him to come back here. Years of work, planning, hoping. Breaking rules, breaking laws.

Making deals with the Mafia.

"And you're with me," he said, his voice sounding like he'd eaten gravel. "I know the circumstances suck, with you being wounded and away from your family and your time... But I am glad you can meet mine."

She nodded, eyes watering. "I know. I'm glad, too." She reached forward and squeezed his knee, and warmth flowed through him.

This woman was everything. Everything he wanted and everything he didn't know he needed.

They passed by two fishing boats, the men in them scowling at him. He recognized one of them, Frogeir, and greeted him. The man nodded in surprise, frowning in confusion to recognize Channing.

They docked and Channing helped Ella to get out. The planks on the wooden jetty were wet from the melting snow and they bent at times.

He offered Ella his arm to lean on, but she shook her head decisively. "I'm fine. I want to meet your family with my head high."

He sighed and took her hand in his. "At least allow me this."

She intertwined her cold fingers with his and squeezed his hand. A warm smile spread on her beautiful lips. He didn't see her smile like this often, and something warm spilled through his chest. "Freya's lips, I'll do anything to see you smile like this every day."

She rested her forehead on his shoulder, the gesture so simple but so intimate a tremor went through him.

"The Norns are cruel," he whispered. "Bring the woman I

want to spend an eternity with into my life only to have the world freeze and die around us?"

She looked up at him and her eyes were wet. "We'll never have an eternity, Channing. We'll be lucky to have one day."

"I'll take it."

He leaned down and kissed her, a soft, tender peck, and when he pulled away, there it was, that beaming smile that made soft waves of electricity charge through him.

"Let's go. Get you warm, hydrated, fed, and have you tended."

As they walked through the village, he inhaled the familiar, wet scent of woodsmoke, animal dung, smoked and dried fish, and hay. The wooden planks of the paved road squelched under his feet, sinking slightly into wet mud. Goats, cows, and sheep called from within the longhouses, kept indoors for the warmth of the families and the animals themselves.

"This is no Boston, is it?" he asked, chuckling. "No Infinity Tower."

She looked around. "It's so Nordic...so beautiful. I like it."

The path towards his father's mead hall led up the hill, and twenty or so feet before the mead hall, the large gate opened and someone stepped out.

Channing recognized her right away.

A crown of strawberry blond hair, a bit more silvery than when he'd seen her last. Back straight, the posture of a confident woman who knew her worth and what she was good at. She held a basket in her hands, and huddled in a long white fox-fur cloak, putting up her hood.

"Mother..." he whispered in Old Norse as everything in his chest tightened.

No one would ever understand fully what connected him and her. They both were strangers here, him less so than her. But they were both from another time and both running away from a terrible man. And the bargain she'd struck with the Norn for him, to respect his choice, to give him a better life, was a bargain with destiny.

He knew her love for him had no borders, and nor did his love for her.

Holding the edge of her hood to see better, she turned to them and watched them approach. She blinked and frowned, her head bent to see better...

Then she dropped the basket and her hands shot to her mouth. The basket rolled down the path, dry reeds knocking softly against the wet wood. Channing bent in time to catch it and smiled the broadest smile to the woman who'd raised him and who knew him better than anyone else.

"Channing?" she whispered.

"Hello, Mother."

"Hakon!" she cried as she sprinted towards Channing. "Hakon, come here at once!"

And as his mother fell into his embrace, wrapping her arms around his shoulders and shaking from tears, he let go of Ella's hand and buried his face in the scent of home he'd yearned for for so long.

TWELVE

Fourteen years... A hard knot ached Channing's throat as he held his mother in his arms.

The gates to the mead hall opened, and Hakon's massive figure stepped outside. Behind him, a young warrior scrambled out along with a beautiful young woman with honey-colored hair done in a long braid around her head.

John and his sister, Mia.

"Who is this?" Hakon narrowed his eyes as he walked towards them.

His mother let go of Channing. "It's your son, Hakon, look."

Approaching, Hakon looked him over, wincing thoughtfully. The time machine was supposed to send him to the year 896, only two years after Channing had left the Viking Age. So, even though for him fourteen years had passed in the twenty-first century, only two years had passed here.

Hakon hadn't changed much. He had the same powerful frame—age hadn't slumped his straight shoulders or thinned his dark hair stricken with silver strands. Perhaps a couple more wrinkles creased his face, but they were mostly hidden by the birthmark the color of diluted red wine that covered the area around one eye, his cheekbone, and part of his forehead.

His gaze was still sharp, his back still straight and proud, and his chest was still massive.

"Ulf?" He stopped before Channing, at the same eye level as him.

Something broke in Channing's chest—an ache, a pull he'd been holding off for fourteen years. The fourteen years he'd told himself he was fine alone, in a different world. The fourteen years he'd told himself he didn't need his family, the closeness, the support he used to have.

The fourteen years he'd been lying to himself.

He'd adored and worshipped this man his whole life. Hakon had been what a man should be. He had honor. Strength. Discipline. He put his wife and his family first, doing everything for them.

And it was only now, seeing his father alive and well and in front of him, that Channing understood he'd lived with a giant hole in his soul for all these years. A hole left by the absence of his family. The hole he'd tried to fill with being a successful businessman. With doing his duty. With teaching Old Norse. Building Viking ships. Sword fighting.

The giant hole that only Ella had been able to truly heal and fill.

"Yes. It is me, Father," Channing said in Old Norse.

"Son," Hakon breathed out, and engulfed Channing in a bear hug. "I did not think I would ever see you again."

Channing clapped his father's broad back. Tears prickled his eyes, but he held them back. Father pulled back and held him at arm's length, looking him over.

"You look well, son, but...older," Hakon said. "Why is that?"

But before he could reply, John shoved his father aside and hugged Channing. It was like hugging a giant. Even though John had been born three years after Channing, now he was the tallest of them all. He even towered over Hakon by half a head.

"Brother," he whispered, "I missed kicking your arse in sword fighting."

He pulled back and hit him playfully in the biceps. John had grown up so much in two years, and not just in height. He must be just seventeen now, but he'd grown into a true Viking warrior, with broad, lean muscles, and a square jaw with sparse brown stubble. He was the image of a young Hakon, just with no birthmark around his eye.

He had long brown hair done in a single braid along the top of his head, with the sides shaved. The braid reached the base of his neck. A pale-blue tattoo of a howling wolf's head was on one side of his shaved head. No doubt, Hakon was training John to become the jarl after him. John was likely drilled daily in sword fighting, archery, fighting with the ax, as well as battle tactics like the *skjaldborg*, or shield wall, as well as sea navigation, negotiation tactics, and trade.

Pride for his brother expanded Channing's chest.

"I missed kicking your arse in everything." Channing chuckled.

His sister, Mia, came a step closer, her eyes wide, looking him over. She took after their mother, her honey-hued hair glistening like polished gold. Instead of wearing an apron dress like women usually did, she wore leather pants and a tunic with a broad belt hugging her thin waist. A scramasax—a short sword —hung from her belt.

"It is now me that kicks his arse, brother," she said.

Channing nodded. "I can see that. I better watch myself, too, sister."

She grinned and threw her arms around his neck. He wrapped his arms around her, pressing her tighter to him. She was his little sister, the girl he'd grown up protecting and taking care of, even though she'd been born only one year after him.

When Mia let go of him and stood by his side, hugging him by the waist, she turned to Ella. "And who is this?"

His family all looked at her, and Ella visibly faltered, just a little bit.

Channing recognized the feeling. When he'd visited her house, even though they weren't together, he'd found himself wanting her family to like him and approve of him. He liked that it was important to her for them to approve of her, too.

He put his free arm out for Ella to come closer, and when she did, he took her hand in his, making sure he didn't touch her wounded shoulder. "This..." He looked at her profile. What should he introduce her as? They hadn't had the boyfriend-girl-friend talk that was a common step in relationships of the twenty-first century. But he'd told her he loved her. He'd told her he'd come to save her.

In his heart, he knew this was it. There wasn't anyone else for him—not in this age, not in any other. He loved her. He lived for her. He'd kill for her. He'd die for her. He wanted to wake up with her in his arms every day of his life. But she didn't know this. And she still hadn't told him how she felt about him. So, how could he explain all this to his family in one word?

"This is my woman."

Ella's hand tensed in his. Mother's eyes widened, and a polite smile touched her lips. Hakon studied Ella with a careful frown. John liked her, Channing could tell. A young pup that he was, he probably liked every female that walked past him.

Mia leaned forward and looked at Ella across Channing's chest. Everyone stared, and Ella's cheeks reddened.

"Hello, everyone." Ella made an awkward wave. "I'm Ella O'Connor."

Everyone mumbled their greetings. "Welcome, Ella," said Mia. "We're very pleased to meet you. We're of course also very curious about how and why you two are here. I'm guessing you are from the twenty-first century?"

"You're guessing right. Boston."

"So, why are you both here?" asked John. "And why do you look so old, brother? Only two years passed and yet you look like you are supposed to have sons as old as I."

Channing chuckled. "It's a long story, brother."

"Why don't we all go inside," Mia said. "You two must be hungry and cold."

"And Ella needs you to look at her shoulder."

"But first food," Ella said. "And water. We're pretty dehydrated."

When they walked into the mead hall, it looked just as it had when Channing left. The windowless hall was dark after the bright daylight. Three long hearths were lit up and fires played in them as well as the oil lamps hanging on the columns with Norse carvings.

Inside, as always, food was cooked on the hearths—cauldrons hung with meat and vegetables being boiled. The air smelled like cooked food, herbs, and woodsmoke. This was the place where the völva had arrived during the feast and told King Harald the prophecy that would change Channing's life forever.

As they walked farther inside, he recognized his mother's tidy and clean approach towards everything. She'd trained servants to boil water for drinking, to always clean and wash the cooking surfaces. In the absence of large quantities of other disinfectants, the cheapest and most readily available was vinegar, and the barely noticeable scent of vinegar had always lingered in the air here.

Warriors sat on the benches at the table and played *hnefatafl*, Viking chess. Female servants spun wool and used looms to make fabric. Others sewed clothes. Children played on the floor with wooden toys. A couple of household cats slept in the alcoves along the walls.

As they took their seats on the benches at one of the tables, it was as though he'd never left. Had that völva not come, he'd still be here. He'd be twenty. Would he have been married by now? There'd been no one he'd liked romantically back then, but many men of twenty years were married and had children.

He was thirty-two now. His mother was forty-seven and Hakon was fifty-one. Suddenly, Channing was much closer to them in age.

Odd didn't even begin to cover it.

"Mother, sit," said Mia as she laid her hand on her mother's shoulder. "Speak to them. I will take care of the food and the drinks."

The older Mia smiled at her. "Thank you, sweetheart."

As the young Mia walked towards the central hearth, Ella took a seat at the table, watching Mia talk to one of the servants.

"You guys have slaves, too?" Ella asked darkly.

Mia shook her head. "No."

"My wife made me free all the slaves," Hakon said. "Some of them stayed and work as servants, for pay. Others decided to leave."

"I couldn't stand the idea of slavery," said Mia, and Ella and she exchanged an understanding look.

Ella relaxed visibly. "I appreciate that. A slave of King Harald saved my life, sacrificing hers. I will never forget that."

"You were with King Harald?" asked John.

"Yes," Ella said. "He captured me."

Hakon shook his head. "The bastard. I regret having helped him become king in the first place."

"What happened after I left?" asked Channing.

"He told me his support had ended. For the sake of our history and what I have done to put him on the throne, he did not punish me for standing up for you. But he stopped protecting Lomdalen and told the other jarls my jarldom was fair game. Over the past two winters, several jarls have attempted to raid us."

John grinned. "They went home with tails between their legs."

Three serving women and Mia brought trenchers of boiled mutton and fresh bread and put them in front of everyone. Then one of them put a clay jug in the middle of the table and drinking cups made of horns. Channing recognized the jug—Mother had bought it from a trader when Channing was thirteen. It was as though no time had passed at all.

"Start at the beginning," his mother said as she poured water into the cups. "What happened when you traveled in time?"

Channing started talking. He told them how he'd looked for a way back at first. How everything Mia had told him about the modern world and her teaching him to read and write in English were helpful. How he was lost in the world where everything worked differently. Where money was God and success was a drug. Where the world operated on information and technology.

"When nothing else worked, I began reading. I read the Icelandic sagas and the myths and legends about the Norns. There was nothing about time travel. But I did find something that broke my heart." He looked into his father's steely eyes and into his mother's soft, dear face. Odin, it was so good to see them alive. To touch them. To hear their voices. "One Icelandic saga told a story of Jarl Hakon and his family who were burned to death soon after his oldest son disappeared."

Silence hung over the table as his parents exchanged long, sad gazes.

"So I made a decision. I'd find a way back and prevent this from happening."

Mia took a sip of her water. "Did you manage to find one of the Norns?"

"No. In a world where technology can do anything, I could hire the best scientists and have them work on developing time travel."

John scratched his forehead. "Mother, is he talking about the flying iron dragons?"

Mia watched him with wide eyes. "No, John. He's saying he decided to invent a time machine."

"Yes. If the Norns didn't want me to travel back in time, I'd find a way to bend time travel to my will."

"How?" asked his sister.

"In the twenty-first century, money is everything. So I needed to become rich." He kept talking. Kept telling them the story of how he started working in the Port of Boston in the lowest position and worked his way up. How he became successful and bought the port. How he built the secret basement and hired two brilliant scientists. How they deciphered the runes and studied the form of the golden spindle mathematically for years.

Until, finally, it worked.

Ella listened to him, too, open-mouthed. She didn't know a lot about his past, so many of the things he told his family were new to her, too.

Then he began telling the story of how they met and how he'd needed to import the nuclear reactor, and how Ella was a Boston cop who was after him. About Náli, Ragnar, and Eirik, who came after him. About the wolves and the roosters and the snowstorms.

How Ella had touched the spindle and disappeared through time.

How he'd been arrested but managed to make the spindle work to find Ella.

Ella told them how she had been captured by King Harald and wounded as she escaped. And how all of that brought them here.

"So now we must find a way to send Ella back home, to the twenty-first century. She has family there who depend on her financially, and without her, they'll lose their homes."

Mia reached out to Ella and covered her hand with hers. "My dear, I can see that my son cares about you deeply, which means you're a good person. You're far away from your family. Trust me, I know the feeling. But I want you to know that you have family here, too."

Ella smiled and squeezed his mother's hand. "Thank you, Mia, you have no idea how much that means to me."

"Good." Mia straightened on the bench and then climbed out. "But first things first. You have a serious wound there that clearly needs treatment. Let's go to my surgery and I'll take a look at it. Then we'll figure out how to send you back."

THIRTEEN

Channing sat by Ella's side in Mia's surgery. He didn't step away from her for a moment, even when Mia had told him to leave when she was looking at Ella's shoulder wound.

She lay on Mia's examination table in her suit pants and the tank top she'd had under her shirt. All her clothes were grimy, ripped in places, caked with blood and dirt, and she couldn't wait to take a bath and put on something clean. The table, to Ella's surprise, had four wheels and stoppers to keep them from rolling. Smart woman, Mia had clearly modeled it after the stretchers in the modern hospitals.

As Ella lay on the table, Mia stood with her back to her, arranging the tools and instruments on her preparation table. She had a neat row of shelves on the wall and four oil lamps that smelled pungently of something like bacon being burned.

"There's not enough light," Mia said as she moved towards the other wall and opened the shutters. Daylight and cold air poured into the room. "It's cold outside, I know, so I'll try to make it quick. That's what I really miss from modern times... good, clear light to be able to see my patients."

She took a bowl of water and a stack of clean linen cloths and put them on the table next to Ella.

"This will hurt, unfortunately," said Mia as she undid Channing's dressing. When she removed the layer of moss, cold air touched Ella's inflamed skin, and pain clawed at her. "You used sphagnum moss I see, son. Well done."

"You taught me all the right things."

Mia smiled warmly at him, and Channing at her. Something stabbed at Ella. Envy, she realized. He had the most wonderful mother in the world who loved him, who'd fought with destiny for him.

Her mother had left her.

She'd never have a moment like that, although she was happy for Channing that he'd reunited with his family.

"Channing, sweetheart, give her the willow bark tea, please. It'll taste awful, but it'll help with pain. It's pretty much what aspirin is made of. There are also other herbs that'll help."

As Mia soaked a clean cloth in the bowl of warm water, Channing brought a cup to Ella's mouth and helped her hold her head. She drank the terrible, bitter tea, struggling to swallow. It did taste awful.

When she leaned back, smacking her lips, desperately trying to get rid of the taste, something warm lay on her wound and burned it. Ella hissed with pain.

"I know, honey," Mia said. "This is to clean it. The burns are bad, but, Channing, you did a good job. Of course, I can't say what's inside, but for now, I don't see any signs of pus. I have a salve to help with the burns, but I think Channing did well."

She finished cleaning and spread something cool that smelled like a mixture of animal fat and herbs on her wounds. By that time, Ella was drowsy. Her pain had been dulled to an echo of the agony she'd been in for the past few days.

"How did you travel in time?" asked Ella.

"A spindle, of course," said Mia. "The Norn, Skuld, in the salad-green dress, she gave me the spindle in Mass General. I woke up at the rune stone that's up the hill from here. Then Hakon grabbed me like a wild bear. I was terrified." Mia chuckled. "Little did I know he's a teddy bear with the people he loves."

Ella looked at Channing and chuckled. "Sounds familiar."

Channing leaned back in his chair and eyed her from under his lashes. "Shut up, woman." A slight grin played around his lips.

"Then when I went back to the twenty-first century, I just touched the rune stone."

"Oh," Ella said. Her head spun pleasantly. The salve was so soothing and warm against her burns. The pain pulsated dully in her shoulder. "So I should try that, right?"

"Gently hold her arm up so that I can bandage her," Mia said to Channing, and he picked up Ella's arm and held it at an angle. Mia wrapped a clean cloth around Ella's shoulder. "Yes, you definitely should try that."

Hope bloomed in her chest. To get back to Dad and Ted and Gloria. To keep working, keep the roof above their heads. To get Dad treated for cancer.

To spend as much time with them as she could.

Channing's green eyes were on her, his jaw clenched, his mouth in a tight grimace. He put her arm on the table so gently it could have been made of glass.

Oh God…it would mean leaving *him*.

Forever. Because he would stay here, with his family. That was what he'd always wanted, what he'd worked fourteen years for. Built the time machine for.

Something in her chest broke.

"Do you want to go right away, sweetheart?" Channing asked, his voice soft, his gaze not leaving her face for a second.

Mia went to close the shutters and semidarkness fell again in the room. She gently touched Ella's shoulder and smiled at her. "As your doctor, I think it would be best for you to get to a hospital as soon as you can. As the mother of the man who clearly cares for you, I'd have loved to get to know you better."

Something melted in Ella's chest. She could see where Channing got his big heart from. Both his mother and Hakon were incredible people. Ella tried to push herself up, but her head was woozy. Mia grasped her healthy arm and helped her to sit. Channing put a fur cloak around her shoulders.

"It's not my shoulder that worries me, Mia," Ella said. "It's my family. As Channing mentioned, they could land on the streets if I don't keep my job."

Mia exchanged a worried glance with Channing, then gave Ella a reassuring smile. "Very understandable. It's still daylight, so we can go whenever you say so. It's a short hike up the hill. Just say the word."

She squeezed Mia's hand and walked out.

Ella looked at Channing. "You're staying here, I assume?"

He looked down at his knees and clenched and unclenched his fist, something she'd noticed was his habit to relieve tension. "I have never wanted to be able to be in two places as much as I do right now."

He looked up at her. "This is what's best for you, Ella. For your family. You'll be safe there. Your family needs you."

Safety didn't matter, she wanted to say. As long as she was with him, she wasn't afraid of anything.

Not the wolves. Not the deranged Vikings. Not Ragnarök itself.

But she didn't say any of that. What was the point?

Somewhere deep down, she knew it wasn't surprising he wouldn't stay with her. Like her mother hadn't.

She hung her legs from the table. "Yes."

He moved to stand between her thighs and gently lifted her chin so she would look into his eyes. "But the gods know I don't wish for anything more than to find a way to be with you forever."

Delight squeezed her core. He leaned down and planted a gentle kiss on her lips, and sweetness spilled through her veins. Combined with Mia's magic tea, Ella was flying. He deepened the kiss, his mouth warm and succulent and tender. He was so, so gentle with her...unless she didn't want him to be.

He wanted to find a way to be with her forever...

If she was honest with herself, she wanted the same.

But there was no forever for them. There would be no forever for her with anyone.

So the faster she could get out of here and rip the bandage off, the better. And it may not work, anyway.

She pulled away from him. "There can't be a forever for us, Channing. Let's just go."

She thought she saw a light die in his eyes as she said that.

It was indeed a short walk up the hill. Still woozy, Ella allowed Channing to support her as they climbed the steep, rocky dirt. Hakon, Mia, John, and the younger Mia all came. The woods were dark around the path, and cold wind blew the scents of pines and wet earth into Ella's face. Somewhere to her right, gray fur flashed between the trees.

"Are those wolves?" John asked, and as Ella looked over her shoulder at him, he put his hand on the head of the ax hanging on his belt.

Channing looked darkly at the woods. "They are."

"Loki's piss," murmured John.

The higher they went, the colder it grew. Tiny snowflakes as sharp as icicles hit Ella's face.

"I hope it works, but it might not," said Mia. "I know the Norns are responsible for opening the portal of time or whatever it's called."

Hakon took his ax and held it in his hand as he looked around. "I do not think it will work, personally."

"That was what you'd hoped for with me." Mia chuckled and playfully slapped his arm.

"Yes, I did. But despite my hope, it sucked you through time and away from me. I had to cross time myself to get you back."

Channing squeezed Ella's hand. "Don't lose hope, sweetheart."

John said loudly, "But Mother is right. If the Norns do not want Ulf to cross time, they will not want Ella to go anywhere, either."

The young Mia said, "But how did Ella cross time, then?"

"Because she touched the golden spindle."

Channing's sister tsked. "But it does not work by itself. Right, Ulf?"

"Right," Channing said quietly.

"So then, how did she travel in time?" pressed John.

As the family discussed the issue, Ella put her head on Channing's shoulder. She didn't want to tell him, but she'd never felt more torn in her life. A big part of her didn't want to go anywhere, either.

A few minutes later, they arrived. "The sacred grove," said Hakon, looking around the clearing, a simple, open space surrounded by bushes and trees. Smaller rocks protruded through grass and moss here and there. In the center of the grove stood the stone. It was a simple, vertical rock carved with runes and interwoven Viking patterns. It didn't look as imposing as the golden spindle.

But something about it…she felt it. The power. The strangeness.

The way.

Perhaps, not even the way. The light shining through the crack in the door.

Whether the door would be locked was the question.

"So, that's it?" Ella asked. "What do I do?"

Mia shrugged. "I touched it with my hand. The rest happened by itself."

Ella looked at Channing. He didn't nod. Didn't say anything.

"Here I go…" she murmured. She leaned to him and wrapped her arms around his neck. He stood like a tree, hard and tense and unmoving. He didn't even breathe.

"Better leave, Ella. I'm afraid if I wrap my arms around you, I will never let you go."

She wasn't sure she could let him go, either. "Goodbye," she exhaled, her breath coming out in clouds.

Just rip the Band-Aid off, she told herself.

Then without giving him another glance, she marched through the wind, blinking off the biting snowflakes.

Don't stop. Don't stop. Don't look back.

His gaze was heavy and hot on the back of her head. If she hesitated for even a moment, she didn't know if she could really go through with it.

She slammed her hand against the cold, hard rock. Her palm stung.

Wind kept blowing at the side of her face. The ground didn't shake and didn't move, and the grass and moss were soft under her soles. The rune stone was still hard and cold and gray under her palm.

She slammed her hand again. And again. And again.

She tried doing that trick, something she did in moments of danger or in her dreams, that reality-stopping thing she couldn't explain. Like when she'd saved Channing from the arrow just a few days ago.

But it didn't work.

Nothing happened.

The door remained closed tight. And, it seemed, she didn't have the key.

She touched the rock with her other hand. She hit it with the side of her fist.

"Ella!" Channing called. She looked up at him. Wind stung the wet skin under her eyes.

"I'm sorry, honey," Mia said. "It didn't work."

Channing walked closer, stopped a few steps away, and lifted his open palm towards her. He didn't insist. He didn't force her.

She put her hand in his.

Part of her warmed up in relief and joy. She wasn't going anywhere. She was still with him.

But her family still needed her, still waited for her. How crazy was she that she was glad she could stay with him longer?

FOURTEEN

Ella sipped hot tea from a clay cup, regaining some of the warmth that this giant house sucked out so easily. She stared into the flames of the central hearth, one of three that ran along the length of the hall.

It was evening, and the hall was dark, save the flames in the hearths and oil lamps hanging on the wooden pillars here and there. The servants and Hakon's warriors were all done with the day and crawled into small alcoves or huddled into bedrolls on the reed-covered floor. The mead hall smelled like stew, fermented honey, herbs, and woodsmoke.

No, this wasn't Boston. There was no running water, and outhouses stood a short walk away from the mead hall. Servants carried water in buckets from the village well to the bathhouse, which Ella and Channing had used earlier this afternoon after the rune stone fiasco. Finally, Ella felt clean. The woolen medieval chemise was soft against her body.

Another interesting thing about the Viking Age, there was no privacy. The only ones who had their own bedroom were

Mia and Hakon. Everybody else either slept in the mead hall or lodged with the villagers.

Hakon was sitting across from the hearth with a cup of tea, Mia by his side. She had, apparently, forbidden him from drinking alcohol several months ago as he was not getting any younger. John and the younger Mia were chewing bread at the table, and Channing was by Ella's side.

Hakon's birthmark gave him a mysterious look, as though he wore a half mask.

Despite her external bravado, Ella was still nervous. She'd never been that girl who was introduced to the parents, and now having Mia and Hakon watch her in that "is she good enough for our son" way was intimidating.

Especially since Ella and Channing both knew this wouldn't be a forever thing.

And they were all discussing what to do. How to send Ella back.

How to stop Ragnarök.

"Is it possible to call one of the Norns?" Ella asked the group.

"I don't think so," said Mia and looked at Hakon. "It never worked when I tried."

He shook his head. "No one can tell them what to do."

He threw a sharp glance at Channing.

Channing nodded and put his cup down on the small table around the great hearth. "If the rune stone isn't working and the Norns aren't cooperating, it may not be possible to time travel without the golden spindle."

"The one that did not work at first," added John.

Ella liked John's straightforwardness. Clearly, he was a kind young man, too. He agreed to give Channing and Ella his own alcove, while he'd share the bed of a pretty servant girl he liked.

"Yes, the one that didn't work at first," said Channing. "But somehow it worked for Ella nevertheless."

"It must be about the runes," Ella said.

"Maybe..." Hakon rubbed his beard, staring at the fire. "Though I do not think even the runes make it possible without the Norns being involved in some way."

"The Norns have power..." said Channing. "My scientists have determined that it literally takes power. Mother, I had to import a seventh-generation nuclear reactor to make the runes work. But the time machine was shut off when Ella—"

He stopped, staring at Ella with wide eyes, his mouth open.

"Power..." he whispered. "You must have had some power, Ella."

Ella's face muscles were numb. "What power?"

Mia narrowed her eyes at Ella. "You know, he's not wrong. If the spindle was there, the runes and everything, but no Norn, then you must have been the catalyst in some way."

Slight pain tightened Ella's chest. No one knew about her dreams. No one knew she thought she could change events. And no one should find out. "I have no idea what you're talking about."

Channing's sister's eyes sparkled. She climbed from the bench and paced along it.

"Think." She folded her hands. "There must be some spell that you used, maybe the same one the Norns use when they make people travel in time. Maybe you thought it? Said it out loud."

Channing put one leg over the bench and turned to her with his torso.

"Yes, you did say, 'Stay here, with me. Let's figure out how to get through this together. If I traveled in time—.'"

Ella licked her lips. The tension in her chest hardened into a ball. "Okay, I did, but what does it mean? We don't know if these words mean anything."

They all were silent, and all four pairs of eyes were on her. Ella fidgeted on the bench. She never liked being the focus of attention.

And what if Channing was right, and there was some power in her that helped her time travel? She sometimes felt like she could pause time and make it go faster or slower, change things...

Like when Channing and she were fleeing from Harald's army. Arrows were raining down around them, thumping quietly as they hit the ground.

Ella and Channing hurried down the slope, and she thought they'd make it.

And then there was this grunt, as though the air was pushed out of him. She looked over and froze in terror as she saw the arrow piercing his back. He was falling, surprised, chest first.

And she'd seen his death...

And she screamed.

And time stopped.

He froze, half fallen, in midair. Arrows hung around them. She could knock them away.

She did that.

But it wasn't enough. She had to change what had already happened. She couldn't let him die.

So, just like in the dreams she sometimes had, she rewound the event. Went back in time. Watched the arrow move out of Channing's body, his flesh grow back together and seal, unharmed. Channing lifted back up into a straight position.

That was enough to keep him alive. The arrows flew to the bows that had shot them.

But the arrow that would kill him was still on its course. She pulled him away from the arrow with all her force...

That had sucked out all her energy, all her power. She was wiped out and he'd had to carry her.

Could he be right? Did she have some powers?

Her whole life, she'd thought she was different from everyone else, a bit odd. But she was never sure why or how. It was always a mystery to her. She covered her oddness with a tough exterior, being distant from people, avoiding friendships and relationships. Keeping her circle of friends to a minimum and caring for her family.

But if it was true that she could do strange things no one understood, what would happen?

Fear struck her, chilling her whole body, making her feel faint.

She didn't need any powers, she didn't want to time travel, and it all freaked her out. Her whole life she'd wondered if her mother left her because there was something wrong with Ella.

And now Channing was suggesting that there was.

No. She didn't need this. What she needed was to return to her family and make sure they were cared for, protected.

With a heaviness in her chest, she stood up. "If I had any powers like you're suggesting, the rock would have worked when I touched it. There must be something else in play here. Maybe one of your Norn things appeared there without us noticing her and activated it."

Channing shifted on the bench towards her. "Ella—"

"Let's keep thinking about it tomorrow. I don't mean to be rude, but I'm going to bed, and you have so much to talk about with your family. Mia, Hakon, thank you for your hospitality."

Under a worried look from Mia, Ella left the table and went to the alcove she and Channing had been given. The painkiller must be wearing off because her shoulder started to ache and throb again. She knew she might have a sleepless night ahead of her.

Good. She didn't want to dream. She didn't want another confirmation that anything was wrong with her.

FIFTEEN

But she did fall asleep and dreamed that she ran along a gravelly beach. The sky was red, and the snow was red, and wolves chased her spilling from the black pine woods from the east. From west, a sea of fire rose like a tsunami, about to crash over the world and burn it all.

"You have powers..." someone told her. "Use them. Stop this."

What powers? There was zero proof she could do anything.

And what she had thought was her manipulating time or whatever...most likely, it was her overactive imagination. People hallucinate things. Maybe she had schizophrenia.

The more she thought that, the higher the wall of fire rose, the closer the wolves came, yapping, howling. She could hear them pant, teeth gnashing at her ankles. The wave of fire crashed with the roar of a storm, coming closer and closer...

She must have screamed.

And then it was over. Strong arms wrapped around her and pulled her out of the dream.

Channing...

She sagged into him, nestling against his hard chest and stomach with a sigh of relief.

"Are you okay?" he whispered, burying his face into her neck. "You were thrashing and whimpering."

She sighed, pulling his arms tighter around her waist. This alcove was surprisingly comfortable. The mattress was soft, filled with goose down, and the blankets were made of sheep's wool, and over everything, a layer of soft fur. She was warm, clean, and comfortable, and even her shoulder wasn't complaining much, or maybe she'd already gotten used to it.

"Bad dream..." she whispered.

She wiggled in his arms and turned on her back to face him. He loomed over her, and she could barely see him in the darkness. Through a gap between two hide curtains, a very pale strip of light illuminated Channing from behind. The only sources of light came from the center of the hall. It was quiet now beyond the curtain; the only sounds were fire crackling in the three long hearths, and people snoring peacefully in the distance.

They were in their own small world now, cozy and shielded from the outside.

Ella reached out and tucked a strand of hair behind Channing's ear. "Sorry I stormed out like that. I hope your family isn't offended."

"No. Just worried about you. So am I."

He was—she could see that in his eyes. That look of worry warmed her, made her feel whole.

She cupped his face with her good hand, caressing his cheekbone with her thumb. "I'm fine." He was so warm, so strong, so handsome...and his hard body was pressed against hers. "Especially now," she added.

Slowly, he leaned down and kissed her, soft lips caressing

hers. His mouth was sweet and hot, and the kiss was gentle at first, meant to be tender. But his masculine tang and the salty scent of the sea, leather, and woodsmoke did something to her. It was as if all her senses became electrified, as if she could feel more and hear more, and taste more...taste everything.

They both felt it, she knew, because as he breathed in, he deepened the kiss, leaning into her, wrapping his arms around her. His tongue dipped inside her mouth, hungry and demanding. Spilling fire in her veins, jolting electricity through her body.

The immediate need for him deep in her body made sweat break out across her skin. Her heart drummed in a violent, uneven rhythm against her chest. Her mind went blank, her only thought to press him tighter to her body, dissolve in him, and never let him go.

He pulled away and looked at her. "Are you well enough, sweetheart?"

She was panting, her breath rushing in and out heavily. "Yeah. Just be careful with that shoulder..."

He growled. "Are you sure?"

"We're in ninth-century Norway. Give me your best Viking."

He laughed softly, his eyes shining even in the almost complete darkness.

"And don't be gentle."

Before he could answer, she leaned into him and sealed his mouth with hers.

They kissed in long, lush strokes, hungry and sweet, making her all tingly and warm. He hardened, and her own insides burned and squeezed in anticipation.

He ran one hand down her body, under the blankets, and found the edge of her long undershirt. He reached under it, dragging the shirt up towards her breasts. On his way, he appreciatively cupped her sex, moaning in approval that she had no underwear on.

A delicious shiver went through her when he had touched her there, and when he cupped and squeezed her breast, she arched into him, wanting more.

He rolled her nipple around and around his thumb, and an electric current of pleasure shot through her whole body.

"I won't undress you, to not disturb your wound," he murmured. And before she could protest and say that she was fine, he added, "But I will enjoy your body fully. These smocks are great for that." He pulled her undershirt up to her neck, making his way down her body, kissing a path towards her sex.

She moaned and arched her back as every kiss left a hot, burning trace on her skin, and her nipples hardened from the exposure of cool air.

And then he nestled between her thighs, and his mouth found her sex, and she was gone. The scruff on his jaw scratched her inner thigh, burning her. The contrast of this and his plush mouth caressing her folds, licking, sucking her clit was a shock of pleasure.

She needed this. She hadn't even realized how much she needed him, this closeness, this tenderness.

Just...him.

When he inserted a finger inside her and made a circle, a shudder ran through her body, she felt herself clench around him and her core tighten. He made a satisfied male noise of approval when she moved her pelvis, matching the movements of his fingers with her own.

"That's right, sweetheart, ride me," he rasped.

"Ah..."

He was taking his time like he couldn't get enough of her taste, and way too soon he brought her to the place where the pleasure was almost unbearable. Her thighs were trembling, and she was so close to the edge.

"Channing...I—"

"I know. Let go, sweetheart," he murmured. "Come for me. You need this."

Like a dam, she opened and let pleasure spill through her, consuming her whole. Her fingers dug into his hair, curling around his strands, as though to hold on to him as she rode the storm of sweet ecstasy, the waves of pure sunlight rocking her senses. She whimpered softly, covering her mouth to muffle the sounds. When the last of the aftershocks left her, she was heavy and soft.

Channing rose and pulled his shirt over his head.

And when she saw his big, hard body, his muscles looking as though they had been chiseled from a piece of marble, her breath caught, and she knew she wasn't yet done.

He wanted to stretch next to her, but she sat up and put one hand on his hard stomach to stop him.

"Ella?" He cocked one eyebrow.

In response, she leaned forward to the knotted string at the waist of his pants. Looking up at him and meeting his dark, surprised gaze, she whispered, "I can't use my other hand, so I have to use my mouth."

He let out a long, growly breath, and she hid a smile. She used one hand and her mouth to undo the knot, rubbing against his erection with her chin in the process. The muscles on his stomach hardened as she did that, and she felt him suck in his breath and produce low growls at the back of his throat. When the knot was free, his pants slid down his hips, only to get hung up on his jutting erection.

"Hmm..." She cocked one eyebrow. "Let me help you with that."

She carefully picked up the edge of the pants with her lips and pulled it along his hard length, stroking him in the process.

He tensed. "What are you doing to me...?"

Then the pants fell, and there it was, bobbing up and down in front of her.

She took it into her mouth, and he sucked in a long breath and tilted his head back. "Oh, sweet..."

She loved feeling him so excited, so out of control. She used her tongue and took him deeper in. The velvety, steel hardness of him was breathtaking. Normally she didn't particularly enjoy giving blow jobs, but this was him...

Her Viking...

The man she was falling for. And with him, she wanted everything.

She moved her head back and forth, caressing him, and as he began moving his pelvis, letting out masculine sounds of urgent desire, she started to get excited with him, the apex of her thighs burning and clenching.

"Ah, sweetheart," he whispered. "Ah..."

She leaned back and, taking his hand, pulled him down so that he lay on his back.

"You're a goddess, Ella..." He looked her up and down slowly. "So beautiful... So mine."

She loved hearing him call her his even if it wouldn't last, even if it was just for now.

She straddled him and directed his length into her wet, aching folds. He caressed both of her breasts as he thrust in, and she gasped as her muscles stretched, submitting to the invasion of his hardness that filled her completely, stretching her to the limit.

They fit perfectly, his rigid flesh everywhere within her. And as he moved within her tender sex, her release began to build. He pounded into her, his eyes locked with hers, holding her in their dark captivity.

Her body shook as the orgasm continued to build within her, hot and furious. Everything tightened, and as a trembling sigh was released from her chest, she came violently, arching her back, her fingers entwined with his.

As waves rocked her, she felt him stiffen and withdraw from her, and as he came on her stomach, she remembered distantly that they didn't have condoms in this century. Her noble Viking was still protecting her with every action.

SIXTEEN

She lay in Channing's arms, breathing in his scent as he caressed her good arm. She needed him. She needed this, and now, lying sated and heavy and feeling so close to him, dissolved in him, she didn't want this to end.

Despite being away from her family, despite being wounded, despite the danger that this man carried for the world and for her, this was the happiest she'd ever been.

Maybe even the happiest she'd ever be.

Would he think there was something wrong with her if she told him about her dreams, about those strange moments where she thought she could manipulate time?

Would he abandon her, like her mother?

Or might he understand her like no one else because he had confided a dark secret of his own, risking his freedom and maybe even his life?

And, perhaps, she did need someone to help her understand what it was that she actually experienced in those moments where time seemed to stop and rewind.

She needed to trust him, but trust was difficult for her. He kissed her temple and turned onto his side, facing her, probably drowsy and about to fall asleep. But if she wanted to tell him about her strange experiences, the time was now. She didn't think she'd be able to gather her strength again tomorrow.

"I need to tell you something..." she whispered, and even though she was warm in his arms and under the cozy blankets, a chill ran through her.

His eyes flew open and he supported his head with his arm, looking at her. "What?"

As always with him, she had the immediate sense that she was his sole focus, that she was the only one who existed for him.

She turned her head on the pillow to look at him and licked her lips. "I haven't told you everything about me and...time."

He nodded, his expression turning solemn. "Tell me now."

She sighed and, as nervousness tightened her stomach, she picked up the edge of the wool blanket and started fiddling with it. "It's not easy to say it out loud. I've never told this to anyone. Not even my dad knows."

"Okay."

"Um..." She cleared her throat. "How do I say this so that you don't think I'm crazy...even though I sometimes think I am..."

"Sweetheart, remember, you're talking to the man who told you he was a time traveler."

"And I thought you were crazy."

He chuckled. "True. Still. Whatever it is, it can't be worse than being the reason for Ragnarök."

"We'll see. So. Here goes nothing." She drew in a deep breath. "Sometimes I have these dreams... And I don't even understand what's happening myself...but it's like I can sort of relive the events that have happened to me and change them."

She paused and looked at him. He was listening with his eyebrows drawn, his eyes narrowed on her.

"What do you mean?" he asked.

"Um...well...I sort of remember the event how it had happened, and then I rewind time, like you'd rewind a movie. And then I can change what I do. And when I wake up and I remember the event, it's the changed version."

He was staring at her, blinking. "Odin and Thor," he murmured.

"And then, I can also stop time in real life...or at least that's what I think is going on. Or maybe I've dreamed of those events and changed them. But there are these moments, like when I'm about to crash into something, but somehow there's this moment when everything around me is in slow motion, sounds muffled, but I can still move normally. Like yesterday, when we were running away from Harald's men, I knew one arrow would get you, and I stopped time and pulled you away from it."

His face went blank, his eyes unfocused. "I remember that moment. I thought that arrow would get me, that I was dead. You saved my life, Ella."

"Of course, I'd do anything to save you. That was nothing. The problem is, I don't know how I do that. I can't always access it—it's like a panic mode."

He nodded. "So I was right. You have powers."

Her cheeks burned. "So you don't think I'm crazy? You believe me, just like that?"

He cupped her face. "Sweetheart, I trust you with my life. When I told you my loyalty is to you, do you think I was joking? I trust you. I believe you. I love you."

Her heart exploded in a wild mix of tenderness and fear.

I trust you. I believe you. I love you.

Every word detonated in her head like a bomb, shredding

her reality into pieces. Who was she if she didn't have her protective mechanism of keeping people away?

Tears blurred her vision. Suddenly she wished she wasn't lying in bed, but that she could stand and storm out, get away from him. "How can you tell me that when our days together could likely be counted on fingers?"

"You don't know that. And I'm telling you these things because they're true. However much time we have left together, I want you to know where I stand."

She couldn't bear it and scrambled back and sat upright, her back against the hard wood of the alcove wall.

He sat, eyeing her carefully. "You don't have to bristle up when someone tells you they love you and trust you."

She pulled the blankets higher up and hugged herself with one arm. "Don't tell me what I have or don't have to do."

He let out a low growl. "Why are you picking a fight?"

Because if you die or we manage to send me forward in time, it will be easier if I'm angry with you than if I tell you I love you, too.

"I'm not picking a fight. We were talking about my crazy dreams, what they mean. What do you think?"

He cocked his head to the side. "I think you're afraid. I think you love me, too, and it terrifies you because you don't want to lose me like I don't want to lose you. I think you just told me so in your fucked-up way."

How could he read her so easily?

Because they were one. Because they were so similar. Because he got her like no one else.

Which was so much worse because it would hurt like nothing else.

I do, okay? she wanted to say in an angry whisper. *And it terrifies me. I'd love to stay and fight with you and figure it all out, how to stop Ragnarök and defeat the crazy king who wants you dead and how to save your life. I don't want to lose you, but I can't be away from my family.*

She didn't say any of that.

She fingered the blanket. "Stop telling me what I feel. You're so bossy. Tell me what you think about what I told you."

He chuckled. "She said bossily."

She pursed her lips to stop them from smiling.

He sighed. "Bristle up all you like. I'm not going anywhere. And if you need to tell me you love me on your own time and on your own terms, I can wait. As for your powers... I've heard of something like what you're describing."

Ella held her breath. He stared into the darkness of the corner of the alcove, his eyes moving from left to right as he seemingly tried to recall something. "Do you know the myth of the Norns?"

"Yes. Three sisters that create and spin fates."

He nodded. "They live in a hall next to Urðarbrunnr, the Well of Fate. That well feeds the roots of Yggdrasil, the world tree that supports all nine Norse worlds."

"Yes, that's what I remember from my research. My mom was into all this Norse mythology stuff, and I read a bit to try to understand her better."

"Normally, völvas tell prophecies they heard from the gods and retell the stories about them, the stories of how the worlds were created and of Ragnarök. When I was a little boy, a völva passed by Lomdalen. And that völva talked about the Norns, which they don't do a lot because usually all folk want to hear are stories of Thor, Loki, Freya, and Odin."

"So what did she say?"

"She said that the Norns see the fates in Urðarbrunnr, and that's where they can change them before they happen."

"Okay. So? How's this something like I'm describing?"

"Well, one of the Norns, Skuld, is responsible for 'what

shall be,' or in other words, 'what goes around, comes around.' And she decides what comes around by spinning destiny in Urðarbrunnr. When she takes the spindle and spins an event in the water rotating it clockwise, it will become the future. When she rotates it counterclockwise, she can undo what has been decided and change it."

Ella hugged her knees with one arm. "Okay...I see the logic here of why that made you think of rewinding, but I'm not sure how this is connected to me and how can I use these abilities."

He inhaled deeply and slowly drew out his breath. "I'm not sure, either. I just think the Norns are at play and have a bigger role than we think. And somehow, you must be connected."

SEVENTEEN

The wind crashed into the mead hall and the walls shook.

Channing looked up from his trencher of bread and smoked salmon. Last night, when Ella and he had made love and talked, everything was so quiet and still. The flames in the central hearth jumped and wavered, sending sparks into the suddenly cold air. Channing exchanged a look with his father, who sat across the long table from him and had just stopped chewing.

There weren't many people in the mead hall. Most people were out and about, doing their daily chores of cutting firewood, feeding the animals, bringing water, crafting new tools and knives and repairing the broken ones. Several women in the mead hall wove fabrics on looms. Servants were cutting meat and cabbage, peeling parsnips, frying fish in the big cast-iron pans over the central hearth. Father's warriors ate at the long table next to Channing's.

"Winter is early this year," said Hakon.

The next gust of wind was even stronger, and the gates of

the mead hall flew open. The wind killed the fires in the oil lamps, blew the floor reeds, and sent the thin, small ones flying through the hall. Sparks and ashes from the central hearth flew into the air and as they landed on the dry floor reeds, fires began burning here and there. People jumped off their seats and stomped on the little flames.

"This is not just winter," Channing said, standing up.

Hakon stood up with him, and they walked towards the open gates. Snow blew into their faces, snowflakes stinging them like wasps. It was hard to see through the white mist, but down in the village, down the slope, the fjord wasn't a still snake of water anymore. Dark waters rose, unruly and violent, crashing into the shore.

Channing frowned. "Is it just me or is the fjord about to flood?"

"Loki's shit..." Hakon cursed and ran to the bench they'd been sitting on and grabbed his bear-fur cloak.

Dark figures were running up the hill through the mist. Mother, Ella, and Channing's brother and sister had eaten earlier and were now in the herb garden trying to salvage any remnants of roots and herbs that they could. And even though it was just twenty feet away from the mead hall, Channing worried.

He turned to his father, who was fastening his cloak. "I'll go and get them."

"Good," Hakon said. He looked like a cliff standing against the storm. He was the man people could always rely on, and his village worshipped him—even though, early on, many had thought he'd been cursed because of his birthmark. "I will go and help the people down by the fjord. Everyone needs to get back to the great hall to wait the storm out. We are stronger together."

Channing nodded. Father went into the hall to ask his most

trusted warriors to go and bring everyone from their individual longhouses back into the mead hall. They disappeared down into the mist.

Some people who lived down by the fjord were already hurrying into the mead hall, carrying children, bringing their cows, sheep, and whatever heaps of things they could carry with them. The mead hall would become the village shelter. They'd need food and water. If this storm would last for days, they wouldn't be able to go outside to get anything, so they had to prepare everything beforehand.

Channing hurried into the storm, blinking the snow away. It was hard to see and to walk. There they were, the dark figures in his mother's herb garden, which was surrounded by a wooden fence. The four of them were bent over with spades and rakes.

"Come on!" he cried through the sound of the roaring water and the wind. "Time to get back!"

Ella straightened her back and shoved some roots into her basket. "We're almost finished."

"Mother, the storm is here," Channing called.

"I know, I know." She finally straightened and looked at him. "Just a little more. If *Fimbulwinter* is really coming, this is the last medicine we'll see in years."

The thought chilled him to the bone. "Okay. Let me help, then."

He bent down and dug up the dandelions with their roots and, without bothering to clean them up, threw them into Ella's basket.

They worked for a while. When the wind became unbearable and stole their every breath, they stopped, picked up the baskets, and walked back to the mead hall.

Once inside, someone secured the hall, but the storm kept banging against the gates. Most of the population of Lomdalen was already there, people's faces somber, confused, and worried. While Mother went to the little nook that was her surgery, Channing looked at Ella. Her cheeks and nose were rosy from the cold, and she was rubbing her healthy arm against her coat to warm it up, her fingers red and swollen from working with the frozen ground and the snow. He hoped she hadn't used her injured arm.

Cows mooed and chickens squawked, pecking at the floor reeds. Sheep and goats bleated. Even the horses had been brought into the hall. They'd be all better off staying together in one building and keeping one another warm, even though the animals would, of course, make the jarl's hall filthy.

"It's worse than in Boston, isn't it?" she asked. Her eyes were big and glistening with worry. "I just hope Ragnarök is gone from there."

He pulled her into a hug and kissed her hair, which was wet from the melting snow, inhaling the scent of snow and herbs and something sweet and feminine. "It probably just follows me whenever I go. Your family is likely fine."

"But yours isn't." She looked at him. "We're such an odd pair, aren't we? Probably no stranger couple has existed in the history of the world. You, with Ragnarök following you like a dog. Me, with weird abilities I don't understand."

Despite the heavy atmosphere of desperation in the hall, he felt the corners of his lips crawl up. "I didn't hear a word you said after you called us a couple."

She cocked her head and sadness crossed her expression. "It doesn't change anything, whatever we call ourselves."

"Exactly. So we can call each other anything, even—"

Husband and wife, he wanted to say. He'd known he wanted to marry her for a while now, that there was no one else for him in any age of the world. But, it seemed, everything was against them...

He hadn't even finished his thought when a yell and a loud bang sounded in the great hall, and he looked up. One of the villagers was lying on top of the long table while the cups and trenchers lay on the floor, food splattered around. Another man stood over him, his fists clenched, his face distorted in a mask of fury. He jabbed his index finger into the fallen man's face.

"Do not dare to touch my cow's milk," he growled.

The other man turned to his side and got to his feet, his hand dangerously close to the ax hanging on his belt. "We must share food! I had to leave my cow down at my house. It is flooded with freezing fjord water and all my belongings are gone! How am I supposed to feed my children?"

"And how am I supposed to feed mine if I give away my own cow's milk?" growled the other one.

The first one didn't reply and just launched himself at the other man. More men threw themselves into the fight, fists flying, grunts and angry yelps of pain filling the room. Even women yelled at each other, stabbing fingers into each other's faces. Children started yelling, and, bothered by the noise, the animals joined.

"Enough!" Hakon's powerful voice sounded through the great hall, and silence hung, only disturbed by the wailing of the wind. "We will all share the food while we are here waiting out the storm. There will be enough for everyone, and we must help each other in this time of need. Not turn against each other."

"It has already begun. Ragnarök," one of the villagers called out. "And like the prophecy said, brothers turn on each other, kill each other. It is only a matter of time—"

"No," Hakon said. "Not in Lomdalen. We will be above this. We will wait for the storm to pass. And if this is Ragnarök, we will find a way to survive it, however long it will take.

Because we are family, and as long as we care for one another, we are strong."

Only, if this was the *Fimbulwinter*, Channing wondered, how long would humanity persist once hunger started and people had nothing to feed their children and loved ones?

EIGHTEEN

The storm must have thundered for a week straight. Hours crawled by, and every day tension in the great hall rose, despite Hakon's and Channing's attempts to placate people.

The wailing wind, the never-ending snow hitting the walls of the longhouse, became like a constant headache at the back of Channing's skull, and looking at the rest of the villagers, it seemed they might have a similar feeling. People sat on the benches and on the floors, staring into the flames or into empty air. Conversations were stilted, voices tense. Fights and quarrels exploded more and more often every day.

He felt it, too—the fear, the irritation—like an itch at the back of his throat. And he could barely control the need to snap at someone. Especially at Ella. Maybe because he was lusting for her like a rutting bull. Maybe because part of him was so angry with her for still holding her defenses up so high. For running away from how she really felt about him.

But he didn't snap.

This storm brought out the worst in people, things they normally wouldn't think or do.

He knew Ella wasn't doing well, either, trapped in the long-house with Norsemen. It was a shock to him, too, when he'd spent the past fourteen years in modern Boston.

He hadn't anticipated what a big shock it would be for him.

It must have been day number seven when the tension and the uneasiness in the mead hall rose to a fever pitch.

They still had some food stored, but supplies were running very low. And the hall must be buried under so much snow that it may not be possible to get out at all.

He sat on the bench, doing nothing, tapping his foot against the floor like a goddamn rabbit. He sensed rather than saw that there was someone behind him.

His warrior's instinct kicked in and in one movement he jolted up. At the same time, he pulled his sword from its sheath.

But it was only John. He held his ax in his hand, his feet set wide apart, his eyes dark in the fires of the hearth.

This darkness had encompassed them for several days already. What would it be like to live in the darkness for three years? That was what *Fimbulwinter* would be.

Eternal.

They all missed sunlight and fresh air. No wonder they were all restless, breathing each other's sweat and smelling each other's piss.

Channing lowered his sword. "Sorry, brother."

But John didn't tuck the ax away. "It is all right, brother."

Channing nodded at the jug on the table. "You want some mead?"

John didn't move. Mead was the last thing on the mind of a seventeen-year-old warrior full of energy, strength, and opinion. Channing knew it because he'd been him. At seventeen, he'd decided he wouldn't go to the twenty-first century. He'd decided his path: to be a great warrior, a great jarl, and a great trader, like Hakon.

At seventeen, he'd known exactly what was right and what was wrong and only his father had any influence on him.

"Tell me something," John said and looked around the mead hall. "Was it worth it?"

"What?" Channing asked, even though he knew.

"Coming back."

Channing's fingers tightened around the handle of his sword. "Of course it was worth it."

"What makes you say that?"

A chill ran down Channing's spine. "The smile on our mother's face. Father's approving hug. Your—"

"Mine?" John sneered. "When you were gone, suddenly I became the most important son. The heir. The next jarl."

Damn it.

John made a broad swipe with his ax around the mead hall. The blade of the ax glinted. Many eyes were staring at them. Men, women huddling around the tables, lying on the ground. Children playing with cats and dogs and wooden toys. The eternal hum of three hundred people trapped in a single space died down.

"I'm not going to take your right to the jarldom, if that's what you're afraid of," Channing said.

John's upper lip crawled to his nose in a snarl. "Afraid? I am not afraid of anything. Least of all, of *you*."

Channing widened his stance and adjusted his grip.

"Stop, you two," someone said.

Mia, their sister, stood to their side. Her scramasax was firm in her hand. Standing with her legs wide apart, she glared at both of them.

"Yes. Least of all you," John said, ignoring his sister. "Because you brought *this* to us."

He waved to the gates with his ax. Snow gathered in the

gaps between the wooden planks and wind howled through the cracks.

"John!" barked Mother as she hurried from another corner of the mead hall, maneuvering between the villagers. "Stop this."

Hakon rose to his feet, too.

"He is your brother!" exclaimed their sister.

"John is right," said a man from among the crowd, rising to his feet, an ax in his hand. "Ulf Hakonson does bring Ragnarök. That was why King Harald wanted him dead in the first place."

More men stood, nodding, making sounds of agreement.

"We do not know how long we have to sit here," John said. "The root cellar will be empty tomorrow. We cannot get to the corn silos outside. What will the children eat? What will you feed your woman, Ulf?"

The worst was John was goddamn right. The rest of the people thought so, too. More people rose from their seats, agitated, all speaking at once.

"What the hell is wrong with you people?" Ella stood up from three benches down the row and climbed onto the table, looking around the crowd. People went silent and looked up at her. "You can't just condemn a person to whatever you think is right. That's mob law. Hakon, there must be some sort of law that protects people like this."

Everyone looked at Hakon, who calmly made his way towards Channing, his face solemn.

"No one will be killing anyone." Hakon stood by Channing and pointed at John. "You do not know a thing, son. If you harm your own brother, you will never forgive yourself. Perhaps it will feel right for one moment. But you will never recover. You will kill part of yourself with him."

It was so quiet, Channing could hear mice rustle in the floor reeds. Hakon looked around. "And same goes for you all.

Harm your brother, your friend, your wife, and you are lost for the rest of your life. You will never forgive yourself."

Actually, it wasn't just the people who were silent. It was a complete silence. No endless, broken *tap-tap-tap* of the snow. No wailing and howling of the wind. No shaking of the walls.

Their assailant was gone.

And with it, the irritation. Suddenly, everyone's eyes were filled with hope.

They opened the gate to discover a wall of snow that fell into the hall. Behind it, blue sky shone, brilliant against the white of the snow. And as though an answer had been revealed to him, Channing knew what to do.

He looked at his father, who stood beside him staring at the snow. "It is only going to get worse," Channing said. "I have to get her out of here. Send her back to her time. And, perhaps, I need to leave, too."

Hakon drew in a deep breath and exhaled loudly. "And go where?"

"I don't know, actually. Anywhere I go, it'll follow me."

Hakon shook his head. "I do not think you can run from it forever, son."

Channing nodded. "I need answers. Need to understand the prophecy better. And since we can't figure out how to send Ella through time, we need to find someone who may be able to tell us."

Hakon looked at him, narrowing his eyes. "What do you have in mind?"

"The völva that brought the prophecy. Do you know where she lives?"

"I do. She was a traveling völva, but she settled on Wolf Mountain due to her age."

"Wolf Mountain... That's two days' hiking, isn't it?"

"Yes."

"I'll go."

"Go where?" asked Ella, who appeared next to him.

He locked eyes with her. "To find the völva that brought my prophecy and ask her how to stop Ragnarök. She might be able to tell us how to send you through time, too."

"Then I'm coming with you."

"What about your shoulder?"

"It's fine. It's much better already. We're going."

They gathered their things quickly: dried meat and salted lard, some oats from the remnants of the food stores, furs, a fire steel, and other things for the road.

The sky was so blue when they climbed out of the snow-covered mead hall, it was painful to look at the amount of white that had fallen onto the world. The snow reached midway up the sides of the houses. The fjord was completely frozen. Channing and Ella put on snowshoes.

"I am sorry, brother," said John, whose ax was now in its sheath.

"I am sorry, too," Channing said. "I never meant any harm to anyone. Least of all you and my family. Take care about the fires, everyone. Remember what I told you about the fires."

Mother stepped towards him and cupped his face with both hands. "We all know that. Ragnarök or not, it has nothing on us because we are a strong family that love one another." She looked at Ella and smiled. "You are part of it, too, dear."

Ella returned a shy smile. She was adorable when she faltered like that in front of his mother, whereas she could take on grown-ass criminals without even blinking.

Hakon clasped Channing by the shoulder. "You can do this, son. You can find the way to stop this. I believe in you."

His sister hugged him tightly. "I will cook skyr for your return."

Channing laughed. "You don't cook."

She chuckled. "Exactly. See how much I love you?"

Channing nodded to everyone. As Ella said her goodbyes, too, and thanked them for their hospitality, he realized it had been just over one week since he'd found his family after fourteen years apart.

Just over a week, and he already had to leave them again. As Ella and he waved to his family and marched up the hill, he kept turning back, trying to burn the four figures standing in the middle of the snow into his memory.

He may never see them again.

NINETEEN

They spent the whole day climbing the mountain. The snowshoes his mother and father had provided helped them to gain speed. Hakon didn't know the völva's exact location, and Channing didn't know how long it would take them to find her, especially with so much snow to get through.

It was strange to see the trees with still-green leaves under so much snow. It looked like it could thaw the next day and they'd have a couple more weeks of warm weather, as often happened here. Second summer, they called it.

But if this was *Fimbulwinter*, there wouldn't be an end to the winter. No second summer, no spring, and no hope.

Ella and Channing climbed the rocky, snowy slopes, walked through the dark pine forests, crossed a glacier lake that had become completely frozen in just seven days. They'd taken enough food to last them for a few days, but on their way, they saw no signs of game or birds—not even Channing's goddamn wolves.

All the wildlife must have traveled south as soon as they could, leaving these lands barren.

They might still be able to fish, but with temperatures dropping prematurely, even fish might migrate south seeking warmer waters.

That was how it all started, and in the ninth century, with no refrigeration, no global transportation systems, and no artificial means to provide light and warmth, people would feel the effects of the end of the world so much faster.

So Channing and Ella had to get to the witch soon, and he needed answers from her. The most important one was how to send the woman he loved back to her time.

The sun was already setting when they finally saw a hut. It was nothing more than a shack, really, huddled between the snowdrifts and under the shadows of the giant spruces.

Channing stopped twenty or so feet before the shack, watching it, panting from a long climb up the hill. "There are no signs of life. No smoke, no tracks in the snow. I think it's abandoned. Our best chance for shelter."

Ella nodded. "Okay. Let me look around first, just to make sure." She proceeded towards the shack, and he heard her mutter, "I miss my gun..."

He followed despite her instruction. The door was jammed by the snow, and it took their combined efforts to clear an area large enough to open it. Inside, it was apparent no one had been here in some time. This must be a hunting lodge for one of Father's people.

Channing could barely stand straight, so low was the ceiling. The hearth was small and the smoke hole above it was partly covered with snow. There was a sleeping bench in the corner and a pile of firewood right inside. A couple of cooking pots, an ax, a dressing knife, and a few kitchen utensils stood piled on the single chest, collecting dust. There were a few old furs that probably served as blankets in the corner. It smelled like earth and old wood. Tiny piles of snow lay by the gaps between the wall planks, and as Channing breathed, condensation rose in clouds from his mouth, just as it had outside.

He turned to Ella. "This will do. We'll get the fire going, and we have our warm bedrolls with us. We'll be fine."

She nodded. "Okay. Better than sleeping outside."

A few hours later, the hole above the hearth was cleaned, the fire was crackling and playing cheerfully, and the field stew was boiling. They collected snow and thawed it, added a few strips of jerky, a couple of handfuls of oats and barley and dried parsnips. Not the most delicious food, but it filled the small shack with the comforting scent of a home-cooked meal. And as Channing looked at Ella, who sat in her polar wolf-fur cloak, blowing at the bowl of stew, he couldn't imagine a place he'd rather be.

He told her how his father had taught him to hunt and fish, how he and John and even his sister, Mia, had gone together and stayed in a shack like this for a night or two, and how that time had defined who he was and strengthened his connection to nature. It had taught him that he could provide for himself. He'd learned how to track animals and how to survive out in the wild. How to start a fire without a fire steel and to find plants, nuts, and mushrooms.

"Back then, I thought that was the man I was supposed to be. I never imagined I'd be a billionaire owning a port and living at the top of a tower made of glass. Wearing thin suits that cost months of a simple man's salary. Driving cars, not horses. Building a time machine."

Ella took a sip and studied him with her icy-blue eyes, golden now in the orange light. Firewood cracked and hummed under the flames. "How is it, to be back here? You wanted to get here for so long, went to such lengths...was it worth it? Are you home?"

His chest tightened as he turned and looked into the fire,

the dance of the blaze mesmerizing. "I don't know. Strange thing, I don't feel that this is my home anymore. I don't feel like I belong here."

"Why?"

"Fourteen years, Ella. I guess this Viking became a modern man."

She narrowed her eyes at him. "You're not a typical modern man, my friend."

"Is that a good thing?"

She leaned her head against his shoulder. "Yes. A very good thing." She looked up at him. Her full lips were so close, her scent in his nostrils. "So it's good for you that you're home."

He stopped breathing.

He put down his bowl. "This is not home." She blinked. There was sadness in her eyes, so much sadness he could drown in it. "You are."

Her eyes watered, a tear gathered at the roots of her eyelashes, and he leaned down and gently brushed it away.

"What are you doing to me...?" she whispered, putting the bowl aside and taking his hand with both of hers. "You're going to smash my heart and stomp on it, aren't you?"

"No."

She brought his hand to her mouth. Her face distorted as she cried, soft wrinkles forming around her closed eyes. She kissed his hand, wetting his skin with her warm tears.

He knew she was cracking open. His tough-as-nails woman with an impenetrable shell around her heart was opening up to him, and she was terrified. He knew it because he was terrified, too.

He grasped her and tugged her into his embrace, rocking her. "In all the worlds, in all the times, and all the realities, Ella, you're the only one for me. I've lived here. I've lived in the future. I've never felt like I had a home, like I belonged, until I met you."

She looked up at him, her beautiful eyes bloodshot, her face wet, nose red. "How can you exist, Channing? There aren't men like you. How can you even be real?"

"I'm real, baby, and I'm all yours. Till my last breath. Till the last drop of my blood. Till the last dust of my bones." He took her hand and laid it flat over his heart. "Yours."

She gave out a tearless sob, like a child after a good cry, her cheeks flushed, her eyes glistening with emotion. "So am I, Channing. So am I."

He couldn't believe his ears. Finally, she'd said it. He knew she wanted him, he knew she was attracted to him and possibly she liked him, but she'd never admitted it directly. He knew it was because she didn't let people in easily, didn't trust anyone apart from a close circle of family and friends.

And her saying this... Something peeled open within his chest, the feeling both aching and freeing.

He crushed his mouth to hers, the need to have her, to possess her, to connect to her suddenly as overwhelming as an avalanche. They came together like two waves, and his whole body crackled as though an electric storm swallowed him. There were those threads of light again, like when they had touched for the very first time, charging soft energy as their lips glided and as he drank from her mouth like he was dying of thirst.

He unfastened the brooch on her cloak, picked her up, and let her wrap her legs around his waist. She held on to him with one arm, and he wrapped his arm around her, securing her for the two of them. He was hard in moments. This woman could just breathe next to him, and that would be enough to get him going for her.

He always wanted her. Always.

Having her had become as vital to his life as oxygen.

But not just physically having her. Simply hearing her voice, seeing her next to him, feeling her soft skin, breathing in her scent. He wanted everything, every tiny bit that he could get. She was soft and pliable in all the right places, her ass perfection, her sex... Gods, he could never get enough of her sweet taste, her scent, the feel of her, all plush and wet and tight.

"I want you, sweetheart," he murmured against her lips. "I want to have you hard, and I want to have you now."

"Yes."

He growled with a smile and squeezed the tight flesh of her bottom. Heat flowed to his cock and it jerked with a burning need. He carried her to the sleeping bench big enough for two, where their bedrolls were already prepared. He laid her down on the furs, and she was already undoing her pants and pulling them down. He yanked his own pants, and looked down at her, spread before him, rosy and bare and delicious.

He leaned down to her sex, but she pulled him up to her face. "Not tonight...I want you inside. As close as humanly possible."

This was it. She was surrendering to him, to her feelings for him, to the possibility of happiness.

To love.

He kissed her, deeply, tenderly, showing her how much he wanted to worship her, to be hers, to make her happy. Without breaking the kiss, he directed his erection against her entrance and slowly pushed in, his nerve endings singing at the tight, hot, sleek contact with her flesh.

When he was inside her to the root, he stilled. "Sweetheart," he whispered, looking into her eyes. Her eyelids were half closed, her mouth open in what he knew was pure pleasure. "In another life, if we had been born in one world, in one time, I'd ask you to marry me and be mine forever. What would you answer?"

Her eyes went glossy, a sweet smile spread across her lips, and she bit her lower lip. "In another world, where there wouldn't be Ragnarök and you and I had a future, I'd only have one answer."

He stopped living for a moment. "What?"

"Yes."

He nodded, unable to look away from the blue depths of her eyes that sparkled with the same glimmer of happiness and hope as he felt.

His wife...

He began moving within her, just the way he knew she liked it. And as worlds and galaxies and times spun around them, outside that little shack lost in the wilderness, he knew they were in their own galaxy, in their own world.

In a world where there was no Ragnarök, where he wasn't a time traveler, and she didn't have any powers.

They were a husband and wife who loved each other and who were having their wedding night.

TWENTY

The next morning, when Ella stepped out of the hunting shack, it was a different world.

Sunrays dancing through the pine and spruce branches bleached the snow blinding white. Water dripped from icicles that had formed on the edges of the roof. Snow crunched under her feet and the air was rich with the scents of thawing snow, pine, and wet wood.

Ella and Channing had had such a wonderful night, and now with the sky summer blue, she wondered if by some miracle Ragnarök was canceled and they hadn't gotten the news yet.

Channing banged the kitchen utensils inside the shack as he packed their things. They had just eaten breakfast—the remnants of their stew, and some salted lard Channing had fried in the cast-iron grill pan. It was the closest thing Vikings had to bacon. She'd eaten it with more appetite than she'd thought she could ever have for fried lard. Living in a ninth-century winter required a lot of calories, and she could already feel her body craving more fuel, especially after a day of walking uphill through snow.

Breathing in the springlike air, sun on her face, she felt warm and light and weightless. She didn't want to go anywhere now. To her surprise, this tiny shack with gaps between the wooden planks and a dirt-packed floor had become her idea of heaven.

Channing had said she was his home.

He was her salvation.

On impulse, she picked up a handful of snow with her good hand and formed a snowball as well as she could.

When he emerged from the shack, pushing through the tiny door, she rewarded him with a snowball right in his face.

Only, experienced warrior that he was, he raised his hand and her ball hit his gloved palm.

She giggled as he gave her a not-so-amused look. She loved his face. She loved his everything.

He was hers. All hers.

He had practically proposed to her last night...hypothetically, of course! And she had pretty much said yes. So, purely hypothetically, they were engaged.

Only, it didn't feel hypothetical. It felt real. And it set hummingbirds zipping about inside her stomach.

He put his basketlike backpack on the ground, his eyes on her, hard, like a predator. "A snowball? Really?"

As he slowly walked towards her, her stomach flipped in a whole different way. Even though she knew he'd never hurt her, the look of him intimidated the shit out of her. She stepped back once, then took another step. He launched at her like a wolf, but gently picked her up, mindful of her injury, and fell into the snow with her on top. A small burst of pain was wiped away with his scent, and the feel of him, long and strong and so male, set a low burning heat between her legs.

"I'll give you a snowball," he murmured, looking her whole face over. Then he kissed her, right there in the snow, and she wasn't cold anymore. And as she put her head on his chest, something cold slid down her spine, burning her skin.

She yelped and pushed him away. Snow, she realized. He'd slipped snow down her coat, right between her undershirt and her bare back.

He fell back into the snow and laughed, threatening to make her heart jump out of her chest. She'd never seen him so carefree.

She hit his shoulder. "You bastard!" She wriggled to get snow out of her clothes.

He stood up, and with the wildest, most beautiful grin, gave her his hand to help her stand. She grasped it and he helped her get the snow out of her clothes.

"Let's go, beautiful," he whispered and pecked her cheek, then reached out to one of the Viking backpacks to put it on his shoulders. How could she remain angry with him when he was like this?

"How's your shoulder?" he asked.

"It's fine. Let's go."

Ella stopped and threw the last glance at the shack. It had pretty much become their tiny honeymoon suite. She wished she could take the happiness she'd felt in there and form it into a charm and always carry it around her neck.

With every step she took away from it, she felt that she might never experience this happiness again.

They kept on walking, and the snow in the woods was thawing quickly. They walked till lunch, took a break, and kept on going. Channing figured out by the sun and nature's signs that they were heading north: moss grew on north-facing sides of trees. He even found a few spiderwebs that had somehow survived the storm—that was south.

They kept going, and the sun began setting, shining at their backs, as they continued northeast. Snow thawing and dripping water was like nature's music around them. Birds came back and chirped here and there, calling occasionally. The air was humid and full of the scent of thawing snow and wet animal fur from their coats and hats.

The sense of spring around them gave her hope, and she saw that hope on Channing's face, too. At the very least, this didn't look like *Fimbulwinter* anymore.

And then Channing stopped so abruptly, she bumped into his back.

She looked over his shoulder, and before them, in the shadow cast by the mountain, was a frozen lake. On the opposite shore was a house. The shadow covering the lake and the woods was so dark, it was as though they stood at the edge of two worlds, coming from the world of light into the world of darkness. The thawing ice crackled softly. Smoke rose from the hole at the top of the house, a stack of firewood sat under an attached lean-to, but otherwise there were no signs of life.

"Do you think that's where she lives?" asked Ella quietly, afraid to stir some unknown threat lurking in the shadows of the pine woods around the lake.

"Yes, I think so," he said. "I think we've found her."

Ella looked from side to side. "Shall we go around the lake?"

"I don't know where it ends, we could end up taking another day to go around it. It's still cold, so we should cross it."

Ella looked at the ice dubiously. "Everything is thawing around us. It's definitely way above the freezing point."

"It's fine. I know how to tell if ice is stable enough. My father taught me as a boy, and I lived in this weather for eighteen years. All I need is a good stick."

He looked around and picked up two dry tree branches

and quickly cut the smaller branches off them. He gave one to Ella and took one for himself. She stared at the ice. It didn't look solid to her. In places, it was white and opaque, in other places transparent and she could see black water moving underneath.

"We need four-inch-thick ice," he said and knocked on the ice nearest the shore with the stick. Ella couldn't say whether it was a good sound or not, but he seemed to be satisfied and nodded once, then stepped onto the ice and knocked in front of him again. "It's fine. Use your stick to help you move, and step carefully so that you don't slip. Keep away from me five or so steps."

"Are you sure it's safe? I can see the water through the ice, and it's been so warm today..."

He took a few steps forward and knocked on the ice three times. The sound came thick and loud. "It's never completely safe, but I know what I'm doing." He looked at the shack in the shadows. "We're almost there. She could be the answer to everything."

With her heart dropping into her feet, Ella followed him, her breath catching every time he took a step forward. Every time he knocked on the ice, she flinched, terrified she might hear a crack and the ice would give way under their feet.

"Hypothermia is a real threat," she mumbled, stepping carefully. "Five minutes and your heart stops."

He turned to her. "I know, sweetheart. I won't let that happen to you."

"I'm not worried about me."

He kept going. Step, step, *knock, knock, knock.*

Step, step, *knock, knock, knock.*

As the sun set, sinking the world into gray dusk, it became colder. Slowly, they moved closer to the center of the frozen lake. Ella could now see water moving through the ice right under her feet, but every time Channing knocked, nothing happened.

The ice didn't crack. The dark, cold abyss didn't open underneath them and swallow them whole.

They moved farther.

They were about a hundred feet away from the other shore when a low crackling noise came. She wasn't sure she'd really heard it. It had come from a distance.

"Do you hear that?" she said, her voice urgent.

Channing stepped one foot forward. "What? The crackling? I already heard it before."

Ella's stomach flipped. "You heard it? Why didn't you say anything?"

"Because it's over there." He nodded with his chin to their left, where the lake and the snowdrifts on the shore were a big golden-amber patch in the last rays of the dying sun. "Ice is still melting there, but we're too far away. I didn't want to worry you."

He looked back down and knocked against the ice again.

But as he raised his stick for the second knock, something snapped under the stick, and a crack shot through the milky surface of the ice under Channing's left foot. He froze with the stick still in the air.

"Stay back," he said softly.

Cracks under his feet fractured the ice like lightning bolts.

Terror paralyzed Ella as the ice separated into narrow sheets under his left foot.

The man she loved waved his hands in the air, trying to grab at something, then sank, and the ice sheet covered the place where he'd just stood.

It was as though he'd never even been there.

The silence of the white world around her pressed into her

ears. She couldn't move, couldn't breathe. Her heart thumped once, twice.

A calm, distant thought came. *If you do nothing, he will die and Ragnarök will end. What is more important, your selfish love or the lives of billions of people?*

She screamed. She must have screamed, or that might have been someone else. She felt numb, as if she were no longer in her body.

Then panic cut through her like knives, bringing her back.

Never. She'd never let him die. She loved him.

Do something! Stop time! Rewind it and grab him and pull him away from that ice!

But nothing happened. In that moment, that special gift of hers where she could stop time didn't come. How did she do it, then? She closed her eyes and concentrated, commanding time to stop. Her shoulders ached. She couldn't breathe.

Still nothing happened.

Damn these powers! What use were they when she had no control over them?

She had to get him out of that lake.

She opened her eyes and let out a long breath.

Right. Five steps away.

She lay on her stomach and crawled towards the ice floe. Ice crackled under her, softly, whispering that it might get her, too.

We'll see.

She was now right before the place where Channing had sunk. She pushed her stick under the ice sheet that covered him. Her wounded shoulder screamed with pain, but she only gritted her teeth.

She lifted the ice.

Channing's head popped from the water and he gasped for air, mouth open wide, eyes bulging in panic, his long hair and the fur of his hood clinging to his wet skin. But Ella couldn't hold the weight of the ice with just a stick, and it slipped back down on him, sinking him back into the water.

"Channing!" she yelled as she pushed the stick back into the crack.

She managed to lift it again and groaned as she pushed it off with her good hand and it fell onto the sheet of ice, which cracked in response.

Only, Channing's head didn't pop back above the surface of the water. His graying shape moved down into the black abyss.

"Channing!" She plunged her good arm down for him, gasping from shock as the cold bit into every cell of her skin.

Her hand found him, and she grasped the side of his coat. Pain tore her arm apart as she pulled him up. He raised his head, mouth open, sucking in the air.

She pulled him up with her good arm, pushing with her wounded arm against the ice, but she was slipping, and he was as heavy as a house. "Come on, help me, pull yourself up!" she yelled.

The ice, the water, and even her damn arm were against her. His coat slipped out of her hand, and he sank back into the water, splashing loudly, then reappeared, gasping, clawing at the ice.

"Come on, help me!" She gripped the hood of his coat again and pulled him. "Push yourself!"

With a groan, he leaned onto the ice with his elbows, then strained to push himself up, but rose only a few inches. He sank bank again, but she held on to him.

No! His heart must have slowed down already, his organs and whole body in shock. The icy waters, the weight of his wet clothes, and the whole backpack full of water dragged him down.

His eyelids were heavy, his skin ashen, and he looked at Ella with milky eyes. Did he even see her?

"Come on, Channing!" she yelled, but got no response this time.

No. This couldn't be it. This couldn't be the end of him—the end of them!

Come on, powers, stop time! She strained again, but several seconds ticked by.

Nothing happened.

Then something flashed in her peripheral vision and the stench of a wild animal filled her nostrils. A dark figure appeared next to her, and when she looked up, she froze.

A wolf stood by her side, panting clouds of condensation out of his jaws. He was as big as a bear, his maw was open, and fangs as long as her fingers stuck out. He was black, his fur thick and coarse like hog's bristle. He turned to her with his milky-white eyes and gave a low warning snarl. She jerked, unable to stop herself, but didn't move.

She didn't have a gun, nothing but a wooden stick that he could easily snap in half with his teeth.

But the wolf didn't jump on her and didn't tear her throat open. It leaned towards Channing, grabbed him by the collar of his jacket, and pulled him up out of the water.

Channing lay on his side, his backpack still on his shoulders. He spat water out, panting. The wolf licked his face and, as silently as it had arrived, sprinted away towards the inky woods like a giant shadow.

The moment was surreal. It wasn't just a normal wolf, one of those that had always protected Channing. It was something else entirely. Could this be Fenrir, the giant wolf from the myths? One of Loki's children who'd kill Odin during Ragnarök? It seemed crazy, but if there were Norns and time-traveling Vikings, if she herself had powers—useless though they might be in this moment—who was to say all the myths weren't true?

But there was no time to waste on reflections. As she darted towards Channing, a white hooded fur cloak hurried towards them from the direction of the house.

Ella looked at Channing. He was pale and shivering. "Can you stand?" she asked.

He nodded and turned onto his side to push himself into a sitting position, and Ella put his arm around her shoulder and helped him up.

The white figure stood under his other shoulder. "Quick, we must get him inside, or he will die from cold," the figure said, her face dark under her hood.

They helped Channing up and slowly, carefully went across the dark ice towards the house. Inside, there was a fire, and warm air bit Ella's red and wet fingers. She undressed Channing, throwing his heavy, soaked clothes in the corner. The hooded figure fetched fresh, dry clothes—a tunic that was too big and pants and blankets. They sat him by the fire and Ella watched him, pale and shivering. The hooded figure handed him a steaming cup.

"Drink this, it is a wild ginger tea with honey." She lowered her hood, and Ella stared into the face of a woman in her fifties. Long white hair was gathered in a single braid that fell down her back, fuzz and gray strands hanging around her face. She had pleasant features, sharp, intelligent eyes, and thin lips.

"I suppose you came to ask me about Ragnarök, Ulf Hakonson?" Her eyes narrowed on Ella and relaxed in a curious, amused smile. "But I never anticipated meeting you. Sit down, we have much to talk about."

TWENTY-ONE

A few hours later, once Channing had rested and the völva had fed them and given them warm drinks, they sat around the central hearth, staring at the fire. Channing's wet clothes, the coat, and the fur cloak hung suspended from a clothesline next to the fire to dry. They'd lost the majority of their dry food because it got wet and used whatever was still edible in a stew that the völva set to cook for them.

The house was small, though definitely bigger than their hunting shack. It was, perhaps, half the size of the longhouses in Lomdalen. There were chickens and a cow that were now sleeping behind a thin partition, and the house smelled like hay and animal dung. There was a single bed next to the central hearth, a table for cooking and eating, underneath was a wooden chest with kitchen utensils. Sacks with grain stood in another corner, and dried fish and meat hung suspended from the strings above the sacks. There was also a small trap door in the floor, which, Ella assumed, led to a root cellar.

Heaps of dry herbs and roots hung next to the dry fish and

meat, and small clay jars and linen sachets lined three shelves on the wall.

It looked like a regular person's house, during the Viking Age, except for a staff that leaned against a wall in a dark corner. Ella thought it had some small animal skulls attached to it at the top, mouse skulls, perhaps, or bats. Apart from that, she couldn't see any signs that this woman was what Vikings considered a witch or a seeress. She had none of the stuff a psychic from her time would have.

The völva was called Åfrid, they learned, and she refused to talk about anything important until Channing felt better.

"Do you realize how close to death you came?" she asked him as he scowled at her, but he said nothing.

She was so right. Ella's heart chilled. If it wasn't for that wolf, and then later for Åfrid, Ella would have lost the love of her life.

But, perhaps, saved the world...

"What was that animal?" Ella asked. "That giant wolflike creature that pulled Channing out?"

Åfrid gave her a long, heavy look. "I think you know who that was."

Ella swallowed. "Are you saying it was really Fenrir, Loki's son? How is that possible?"

"How is it possible that you have traveled through time, dear?" Åfrid narrowed her eyes at Ella and smiled sweetly. "And are you saying you never had strange dreams?"

Ella was at loss for words.

Channing set aside the empty bowl. "Let's talk."

He spoke Old Norse now, and Ella allowed herself a short moment of enjoying the sound of his deep voice saying the hard, melodic words.

"You should lie down," Ella said.

"Don't fuss over me. I'm fine."

The völva cocked her head to the side. "You are not fine, Ulf Hakonson. You are far from being fine. You will only recover by tomorrow at this time and might be able to return to your village the day after. If you go sooner, you will not be able to complete your journey back to Lomdalen."

He tightened his jaws. "All right, then. More time to find out the truth. On my eighteenth birthday, you came to my home and told people I would be the cause of Ragnarök. You turned my whole life upside down. You made me go through time when I did not want to. You made King Harald chase me, send his warriors to the future. It's because of you that this woman is here, where she does not belong. How do you know I am the reason for Ragnarök? Tell me about that prophecy. How do we stop the end of the world? And..." His voice broke and when he resumed talking, it rasped. "Do you know how to send Ella back to her time? I need to make sure she's safe."

The völva's clear, intelligent eyes lay on Ella. "Ah, yes. Her. The pair of you, two people from two different times who belong to neither. How interesting that you found each other."

"Interesting that we found each other..." Ella murmured. "What do you mean?"

"It means, you are more connected than you think."

Ella shook her head. "I'm still confused. Is it about the prophecy? Tell us everything from the beginning."

The völva sighed and picked up a bowl of gray wool and rolled fresh wool onto a spindle.

"Tell us about the Norns," whispered Ella.

"The Norns..." Åfrid shook her head once as she attached loose fiber to a string on the spindle, then flicked it and it began whirling, creating a perfect string of yarn. "The Norns are sneaky ladies. One cannot control them, influence them, or negotiate with them. They decide everything. Somewhere at the roots of the world tree, Yggdrasil, one of them has woven the tapestry where I talk with you both. It is all decided before any of us are born, even the fate of the gods." She spun the spindle again, and fiber twisted, thinning into yarn. "Ragnarök, the prophecy all Norsemen have been told since we were children. The Norns wove the end of the world the moment it was created."

Ella kept watching Åfrid's moving fingers. There was something so soothing, almost meditative about this process, and her fingers tickled, aching to try it.

Channing's jaw muscles bulged and worked. "How am I connected to it exactly? Did you see me in your vision?"

"Yes. The vision came to me one night. You, Ulf Hakonson, with a giant spindle of gold, the runes, and some objects I couldn't even describe. Like a white cooking pot as tall as a house, and made of iron."

"The nuclear reactor..." whispered Channing.

The yarn on the spindle was growing thicker as the völva kept working. "Golden threads flying through air, charged like lightning. Wall of fire behind you, wolves tearing the throats of men, people fighting, killing each other, blood flowing, so much blood... *Fimbulwinter*, so early and so strong that it killed all food. And you. You are at the root of it all. You, who decided that you can defy the most powerful beings in the whole world —the Norns. Even the gods fear them and respect them, and yet you thought you could do what you want."

Her voice rang, vibrating with anger and meaning like a tuning fork, and a chill ran through Ella.

"I did think that," Channing acknowledged, his voice low. "How is that the end of the world exactly?"

"Because you cannot fight destiny. Destiny will always win. Your machine, it is unnatural. It goes against the laws of time. You tried to explain magic, to pull apart the sacred, to use it for your advantage. You are an outsider. If you were a real Norseman, you would know how sacred Norse magic is."

He shook his head. "Okay. So you saw that as long as I live, the world will end."

She nodded, letting the spindle drop and then spinning it again. "Yes. That is what the Norns spun in the tapestry of destiny."

"You've seen the tapestry?" asked Ella.

"I have seen the tapestry. I heard one of the Norns whisper it into my ear. I was told to find King Harald and tell him the prophecy."

Channing straightened on the bench. "So why didn't you let me die out there on the lake? Why are you feeding me and why are you giving us shelter?"

"Because I was not told I am the one to kill you."

"Do you know who's going to kill me?"

She nodded and her gaze clawed into Ella.

Silence hung in the small house, and a chill dripped down Ella's spine. "Me?" she whispered.

The völva looked back at her yarn. "You two are the strangest pair. And you"—she pointed the spindle at Ella—"have a much bigger role to play in all this than you think."

Shock washed through Ella like a wave of icy water. "I don't understand. I don't want to kill him... I...I love him."

Channing looked at her so fast, she thought his neck would crack.

"You love me?" he whispered.

Ella looked at her hands. "I know I'm not supposed to. I know I shouldn't let myself love you. I know you can't be with me...but yeah. I do."

He pushed his blankets off his shoulders and pulled her into his embrace. "I love you, too," he whispered into her ear, his breath hot but his skin cool. "Don't listen to her. You won't kill me. We'll defy anything in our way."

"You will not, Ulf Hakonson. And you..." The völva pointed the spindle at Ella again. "You have power you do not want to see. You have power that could save the world...or ensure its destruction."

How did the völva know all of that? She wanted to agree with Channing, and tell him that he was right, that they would defy everything. That was what a modern person would think, after all. All those stories of destiny and fate were just myths, an old-fashioned way to look at life. Modern people knew they were building their own destiny and responsible for their own fortune.

After all, it was all about what people believed about them-selves and the world. If they believed in themselves, they could achieve anything.

But deep down, Ella knew this woman didn't just come up with stuff, didn't throw out suggestion after suggestion until the person gave a confirmation the way most modern psychics did.

She just knew.

"The truth is in your blood," said the völva, looking into Ella's eyes. "Seek the truth in your blood."

"What does that even mean?" Ella asked. "Like literally spill my blood and look at it?"

The völva returned to her spinning. "Of course not."

"Then what?" Ella asked.

The völva didn't say anything.

Channing began shivering again, and Ella pulled the blankets and the furs on top of him. "Can you at least tell us how Ella can return to her time?" he asked.

"I do not know that."

TWENTY-TWO

They spent the night and another day with the völva, but she refused to tell them anything more about the prophecy or her visions. She took care of Channing, and as payment for her service, sent Ella ice fishing because it had become colder again, and the ice had thickened.

The völva cut out a hole with her ax and showed Ella how to fish with a line. Ella sat out in the cold on a small bed made of pine branches, which were surprisingly insulating.

To her delight, she caught two trout, and the völva was happy with her payment. They ate a fresh, rich trout stew that evening, and Ella could see Channing regaining his strength and energy.

On the third day there, he said he was ready to leave, and with the völva's curt nod, he left the house. But the völva caught Ella by the arm. Looking straight into her eyes, she said, "The answer is in your blood."

A chill ran through Ella's veins, as if her blood buzzed in response. But before Ella could ask her anything else, the völva closed the door.

They traveled back in silence. Channing walked in front of her, the stick in his hand, his shoulders slumped, clearly thinking about something.

How she'd kill him, no doubt. Which, of course, she never would. She'd rather die herself. And that destiny stuff... She agreed with him—people defined their own destinies, and how could the Norns be so angry with him for building the time machine when so many people every day lived by the same rule, that they built their own fates?

But still...

The answer was in her blood... Blood... Could she mean her blood as in her parents, her ancestors? Her dad was Irish, and her mom was Norwegian and made tapestries of Ragnarök.

Could her mom be a time traveler, perhaps, sent by the Norns into the future to find the love of her life, Bryan O'Connor?

And if Ella would play a bigger role, if she would save the world or ensure its destruction, she had to understand better what was going on with her.

It was when they got back to the hunting shack they had used a few days prior that Ella knew the völva's words had forever changed her and Channing's relationship. They entered the shack, and he set about lighting the fire in the hearth. Ella spread the bedrolls and went to gather snow to thaw for the stew and drinking water.

When she returned, a fire was playing in the hearth and Channing stood staring into it. She put the cast-iron pot over the fire and sat by his side on the bench.

"How do we keep looking for a way out for you when this was our last hope?" he asked.

"We don't," she said.

"What?"

"I don't want to leave anymore, Channing. I must stay here and uncover the truth about my blood and my powers."

"Ella—"

"I think she meant my blood as in my relatives, probably my mother since she was Norwegian. I think maybe my mother was a time traveler, too, like your mom. My mom must have come from this age, met my dad, and fallen in love like your mom did with Hakon. Only, something must have happened that made her leave. Or she couldn't stand life in the modern world anymore. Maybe she was a Norse witch from the ninth century and that's how I can do weird things with time. Maybe I don't change the past at all like I think I do. Maybe in reality, I see the future like one of those völvas, and then I change it."

He shook his head. "No, Ella, you can't stay here. Whatever mystery there is, you can't stay. You'll die. It's way too dangerous."

"It's not more dangerous than before."

"Yes, it is. She just confirmed that I'll be the destruction of the world."

"Or I," she said. "My gift could be the end of the world."

"Nonsense. You're leaving. End of discussion."

She jumped up to her feet. "End of discussion? It's not up to you, Channing."

He didn't even look at her, the bastard. Kept staring into the fire. "Yes, it is."

"Excuse me?"

He looked hard at her. "I swore my loyalty to you. That means I'll do anything to protect you, even if that goes against what you think is best for you."

His eyes were two bottomless pools of darkness.

"You're kidding me, right?" she scoffed. "I'm not ready to leave. I know the answer lies here, in this time. I know it's close. And I could save the world, that's what she said."

Or ensure its destruction...

"Ella, I don't understand why we're arguing about this. There's no way for you to leave that we know of, anyway."

"But if there was, I'd stay here until I was ready to leave."

"No, you wouldn't."

She shook her head in disbelief. "You're serious, aren't you?"

He turned to her. "Dead fucking serious."

Her eyes burned, tears stinging. "A few days ago, you proposed to me. Yesterday, you said you loved me."

"I meant every word, still mean it."

"But do you understand that you're being controlling? That you're disregarding my right to decide for myself?"

He took her by the shoulders, hurting her wound, his eyes so intense it was hard to look into them. "I don't care. I'll disregard anything as long as you live."

She freed herself from him, hurt spreading in her chest like poison. "Then you're not the man I know. Or want."

The pain in his eyes made her want to crawl into a ball and weep. "What?"

"I'm not going to be with someone who doesn't respect my decisions. It's my life, not yours. I've wanted to know who my mother was my whole life. I need to understand my gift. And I might save the world, and you're barking commands at me like I'm your dog. It's my life, and my decision, and if I want to risk it, it's my business. Not yours."

His jaw worked. "Ella, I couldn't live with myself if I let harm come to you."

"But you can't make those decisions. We'll never work if you want to decide my life for me."

He hung his head between his shoulders. "You're forgetting, Ella. We were never going to have a future, anyway."

TWENTY-THREE

The next day, Channing and Ella reached Lomdalen. The village spread down the slope below, the fjord, still frozen, behind it.

But something looked very wrong about Lomdalen. Too many people, Channing realized.

"Channing," Ella said, stopping by his side. "What's going on?"

"I can't see from here who they are…"

But he doubted they were friends.

As they descended the slippery path in the snow, he concentrated at the task at hand—to not slip and break his neck—and ignored a dull pain in his chest from their conversation yesterday.

She was so unreasonable. How could she worry about him being controlling or deciding things for her when the most important thing was her life? Keeping her alive, sending her somewhere—anywhere, as long as it was safer—was all he cared about. And he hated that she thought he didn't respect her choices, because he did.

Only if it was about her safety, he'd do anything.

Anything.

Because even a life without her by his side was better than a life with her dead.

The snow had melted from the thaw a few days ago but had frozen again, forming a thin crust of ice, and they had to hold on to the branches and the bushes as they descended.

When they could see and hear people well enough, he pulled her to hide behind a boulder. She sank to her knees by his side. They hadn't made love last night like they had on that happiest night of his life, when she had said yes to his hypothetical proposal.

Unlike that night, the sense of Ragnarök was back. In fact, he wondered if that itch, that irritation was partly the reason for their argument. For it to go so badly he felt she didn't want to be with him at all, even though she'd never said the words.

He peered from behind the boulder. In front of his father's mead hall, he could see people gathered. His father, his mother, and his brother and sister were there as well as Father's most trusted warriors. They were facing several other warriors, axes and swords in their hands.

And in front of them was a tall, mighty man with a red beard and red hair, a beautiful sword in one hand, and something else in the other, something that Channing couldn't see.

"Harald..." Ella whispered.

"It was only a matter of time for him to reach Lomdalen. He always knew where I'd go. The storm must have stopped him, and the snow slowed him down, but we all knew, sooner or later, he'd come. Father was ready."

"I know. Still."

They were arguing. His father's shoulders were tensed, his mother's back was so straight he could tell she was terribly afraid and didn't want to show it. His brother was clenching and unclenching his fists, his sister holding her bow with both hands. Harald gestured broadly with his sword around the village.

"I bet he's asking where to find me," Channing said.

"What's our plan here?"

"Stop Harald."

"How?"

Channing pulled his ax out of its loop.

"Kill him?" she said. "Come on, don't be such a Viking. Can we not just restrain him or something? Put him in some sort of jail?"

"I never said I wanted to kill him, and I don't think restraining him will keep his allies away. Remember, he's the king of Norway, all the jarls are under his command and swore loyalty to him. So did my father, by the way."

"So did you?"

He nodded. "A long time ago. But if everyone thinks of my father as someone who breaks his word, all the respect he has earned and the friendships he has made with other jarls will be lost. He will have a hard time trading, and no one will help him and protect him against raids."

"Well, I'd rather have that than you dead."

He looked at her, her eyes translucent and burning. "I didn't think you cared," he whispered. "Not after yesterday."

"Of course I care."

Goddamn woman. One moment she had him all melting and warm and fuzzy like a teddy bear, the next she stomped on his fucking heart. And then with just a few words, she resurrected him again. If anything, she had full control over him. She was his reason to breathe, to keep going, to try to find solutions.

There was another option to stop Harald, of course. To give himself to him. To save his family and the woman he loved. And then to kill Harald. He didn't have to say it to her out loud, but if Harald was dead, Channing would have time to figure out what to do before more people would start to hunt him—which they would. The rumor about him and Ragnarök was out there. And Ragnarök would only get worse.

But he didn't have time to say a word or do anything because a loud pop sounded, sending crows and ravens flapping into the air, croaking loudly.

Channing saw now that the object in King Harald's other hand was Ella's gun. Harald stared at the gun in fascination while Channing's father lay in the snow, blood flowing around him. His mother screamed, fell to her knees. His brother and his sister launched themselves at Harald, their weapons raised, but were restricted by his warriors.

And Channing... Shock hit him like a concrete wall, and he was numb, unable to hear anything, see anything, unable to think. His father, big and strong, and always the source of wisdom and solutions, was now completely immobile.

Dead?

No, impossible.

And then it got worse. Harald's warriors began pushing Hakon's people into the mead hall. His mother, his brother and sister, his sword-brothers, everyone was shoved into the building. The gates were closed, blocked by the hoes and pitchforks. The people banged against the walls and the gates from within.

Some of Harald's men went into the other longhouse and returned with burning pieces of firewood. They threw them onto the thatched roof of the mead hall.

The saga...

Fire consumed the dry thatch hungrily, and thick black clouds rose from the roof.

"No!" Channing screamed. "Stay here," he commanded Ella as he stood from behind the boulder.

But of course she rose and hurried down the path with him.

He had to get them out. He couldn't have his family and all those people burn to death in the mead hall. If Harald wanted him, here he was.

"Stop!" he screamed as he ran, tripping, falling into the snow. "Open the gates! I'm here."

Harald looked in Channing and Ella's direction, and a satisfied smile spread on his face. Channing ran to the great hall to remove the hoes and pitchforks and let people out. The scent of burning wood and thatch was thick in the air, a sickening, strange odor combined with the scent of snow. Ella fell to her knees before Hakon.

"Someone, get me a cloth or something!" she yelled.

Many strong arms grasped Channing and stopped him. Inside the great hall, people kept banging and yelling to be let out. The screams wrenched Channing's heart and he wanted to pull his hair out.

He wriggled out of the arms that grasped him and swung his ax around him, hitting warriors' arms, sides, not really seeing anything as desperation clawed into him.

But there were so many of them, and he was just one. Warriors surrounded him, axes and swords glistening as they flashed, blades sharp and close, aiming to kill him. He fought, knowing this was desperation, knowing this would just buy him time.

Then a howl came, then another and another. And a pack of wolves poured into the village from the woods high up the mountain. Their gray and brown pelts flowed like a wave of fur.

His loyal wolves. They clashed with the warriors. Fangs flashed, and the air filled with the desperate sound of woofs and yaps mixed with plaintive yelps as they were hit. Channing fought together with the wolves, like a force of Ragnarök.

His muscles burned as he kept wielding his weapon. His breath caught, his lungs aching. He was hit once, twice, three times...then he lost count. His heavy parka was as thick as armor, and it saved him from several bad wounds. But it also slowed him, tugged him down, restricted the free swing of his arms.

He didn't know how long all of this had lasted when he saw that the ground was covered with dead or wounded furry bodies. The last few wolves fought with the remaining men. Half of the roof was on fire, and Channing knew that soon it would reach the point where people would start burning alive.

"Ulf Hakonson!" came a belly-deep cry, and Channing glanced to his side. He was still fighting one of Harald's men.

Harald had Ella. He was pressing the gun to her temple.

"Stop," Harald said.

Channing stopped. He stepped back, holding his ax before him. The man he'd been fighting froze, too, holding his sword. The rest were now still. Many of Harald's warriors lay dead, killed by Channing or the wolves, but there were many more—two hundred, perhaps.

"You have already lost," Harald said. "You know what I need you to do. Give yourself up and I will not harm this beauty."

TWENTY-FOUR

"Don't listen to him, Channing," Ella said. "Don't you dare—"

But he didn't look at her. He stared at Hakon, his eyes hard, his face solemn. "Yes," said Channing. "I will."

"No!" she screamed, fighting against Harald's strong grasp. Her shoulder was killing her, pain tearing her apart. She was pressed hard against his chest, his arms as strong as goddamn tree trunks.

Channing pointed with his ax at the burning house. "If you open the gates and let the people out, I will give myself to you and let you kill me."

Her stomach dropped. "No!"

"Ahh, finally," Harald said. "A deal that is reasonable."

Channing swallowed hard and met her gaze, his eyebrows a straight line. "And let Ella go."

Harald's chin touched the top of her head as he nodded. "Of course I will let her go. She is not going anywhere, anyway."

"The hell I'm not..." she growled.

Harald pushed her off him and opened his arms, releasing

her. She pivoted and with her good fist, punched him in the nose. Her fist burst in pain. The punch wasn't as strong as usual because of her bad arm. He groaned, held his nose, and laughed.

"I'll show you how to laugh, you sick arsonist," she murmured and hit him in the eye.

"Restrain her already!" Harald said through laughter, his voice half angry, half amused. "The woman has fire. I am telling you, I am in love with you already."

Two men grasped her, and she beat against their arms, spitting curses and yelling.

"Let her go!" Channing roared as he walked towards them with his sword pointed at them.

"Open the gates," said King Harald, and Channing stopped.

The guards removed the hoes that blocked the gates. As they opened them, people poured out of the house, coughing, gasping. Ella almost jerked out of the guards' arms when she saw Mia and Channing's brother and sister run out of the house, but they held her too well. Mia landed on her knees by Hakon's side, tore her dress, and, launching into fits of coughing, pressed the fabric against the still-bleeding wound on his chest.

"You bastard," Mia spat out, looking at Harald. "He was your ally since day one. He put you on your goddamn throne."

Guilt crossed Harald's face for a moment. "I regret this, Mia, you know I do. I respect and love Hakon. But some things need to be sacrificed so that the world will go on." He looked at Channing. "Bring Ulf to me," he said to the guards.

They grasped Channing and pushed him forward. He stumbled as he walked over and between the bodies of the wolves. His eyes locked with Ella's, and they weren't panicked or full of fear.

They were full of love and conviction.

"No..." she said, pulling against the arms of the guards. "No! Leave him alone!"

Harald's other men brought a stump for cutting firewood and placed it before Harald.

Ella kept screaming. "He may not be the reason for Ragnarök. It may be me!"

Harald shook his head once and turned away. "Do not talk nonsense, woman. The prophecy is clear. As long as Ulf Hakonson lives, the world will sink into Ragnarök. And I will be the one to stop it."

They pushed Channing down so that he knelt and pressed his head against the surface of the stump. King Harald took the ax with both hands and stared at Channing like he was a cow for slaughtering.

"Do something!" Ella yelled at Mia and her children.

But Mia was sobbing, holding the cloth to her husband's wounds, the only thing she actually could do now to save someone. John, still coughing, was thrashing as he was held by an enemy warrior, and Ella saw blisters on his neck. His sister, Mia, was lying on the snow, breathing in asthmatic gasps. Good God, she might have lung damage.

No one could do anything. Hakon's warriors were all coughing and gasping, weaponless and too weak to fight.

Ella went numb. This was it. No one would stop the ax in King Harald's hands. No one would save the life of the man she loved.

She was about to lose him.

Fear gripped her like ice. Her heart beat so violently all she could hear was her pulse thumping against her ears. Harald raised the ax high above his head, his face an impassive mask, a man on a mission to free the world from the evil.

The ax fell.

No! Not Channing.

There was a pull within her.

The ax stopped one inch away from Channing's neck. Everyone around them froze like statues.

She breathed, holding on to this moment. As long as the ax was away from Channing's neck, she couldn't let time slip from her grasp.

Her powers, again.

But how long would she be able to hold this? With her heart beating so fast she might be on drugs, she freed herself from the two men and ran to Channing.

A figure appeared next to him, and Ella stopped, frozen to the ground. It was the old lady from the shore, with the same icy-blue eyes and friendly smile. A green Viking dress. A white braided crown around her head.

But the image lasted only a moment. The old lady began to melt, float, and change like milk dropped into water. Instead of an old woman, a young woman stood before Ella. Blond with blue eyes and a pretty Nordic face. A salad-green sundress.

And a sweet scent of herbs, the woods, and something dusty. The scent she remembered from her childhood...

Her mom.

Shock hit her in a piercing, freezing wave, and the ground shifted under her feet. In her mother's hands, something glistened, and when she stretched her hand out, there was the golden spindle, engraved runes on its smooth surface moving and shifting and floating into one another.

The truth is in your blood. The völva's words sounded in her head.

She was the daughter of a Norn.

But even beyond that, here stood the woman she'd thought about every single day. The mother she'd missed her whole life. The reason for her daily struggle, the reason she thought she wasn't good enough for her mom to stick around. That sooner or later, everyone would leave. That she couldn't trust anyone.

"Mom..." she whispered. "Why did you leave me?"

The woman's eyes watered and she cocked her head. "We don't have much time, sweet. You are part Norn, part human. You can change things and change tapestries. You can now decide what will happen to the world. What do you want to do?"

You have power that could save the world...or ensure its destruction.

There it was, her choice. Go back to her time, let the ax fall, and save the world.

Or push the ax away and take Channing with her.

Ella took a sharp breath. "I want to talk to you."

"My sisters are coming. I can't stay much longer. Now, Ella."

Her mother was dissolving in the air like mist. Sadness and joy, panic and anger mixed boiled in Ella.

Fuck the end of the world. Letting Channing die was never an option.

She grasped Channing's shoulder with one hand and the spindle with her other, aching hand. As her hands brushed her mother's palm, she looked into her eyes again.

And like the last time she'd seen her mom, she had so much sadness and guilt in her face...

And love. Oh, so much love.

Still holding Channing's shoulder, Ella sank into darkness.

TWENTY-FIVE

Daylight hurt Ella's eyes through her closed eyelids, and she squeezed them tight, willing it to go away. It was cold, and she'd just been in such blissful oblivion—somewhere peaceful and dark, where the absence of any sensations, sounds was a relief. Here, it smelled like wet asphalt, gas, and metal. Something chemical, something burning like an oil factory.

She hurt all over, and it was the pain that finally made her sit up and open her eyes.

She sat on a wet road. Port cranes loomed silent and still over her head, and the ship *Naglfar* was docked about twenty feet away, like a dark mountain. The sky was blue—almost summer blue, bright and cloudless. There was no snow, and the ocean splashed quietly against the quay.

Channing...

Still sitting, she looked around and saw him—he was five feet away from her, still in his Viking fur cloak and coat, pushing himself off the ground and shaking his head.

Alive.

Safe.

Relief injected a burst of lightness through her nerves. She scrambled off the ground and rushed to him, helping him to stand.

"It worked," she whispered. "God, Channing, it worked!"

How much time had passed since she'd left? How was her dad? Ted and Gloria? So far, this age looked much better than the age she had left her family in—was this true? Were they okay?

Channing blinked at her, frowning in confusion. The next moment, he pressed her against his chest.

"I traveled in time..." she whispered into his warm neck, inhaling his scent. "I saved you."

And the fact that she had met her mother...her whole being contracted from the thought.

Her mother...the Norn.

Was it all real? In the cold reality of the twenty-first century, it was hard to completely believe everything that had happened. Had she not dreamed it all?

Channing took her by the shoulders and held her at arm's length. His green eyes were cold and worried. "How?"

"I'm still not sure. What the völva said... 'The answer is in your blood'... She was right."

"What does that mean?"

She looked up and to the northwest, across the blue of the Atlantic. An airplane flew in the sky, tiny and silent, leaving a white trail behind it. What a sight...quite shocking after only a few weeks spent back in time. There were cars here, and telephones, and medicine...

And the time machine.

She looked at him. "When Harald was about to kill you, something happened."

"I figured. One moment, I was about to meet the Valkyries. The next, I was here."

"I stopped time. And one of the Norns came."

"Shit."

Her eyes watered and the explosive mixture of joy and loss and anger boiled deep within her. "My mom, Channing. She was my goddamn mom!"

He blinked, let her go, took a few steps back, and ran his hand down his long hair.

His eyes were wild. "One of the Norns is your mother?"

She couldn't see him that well anymore, her vision blurry. She sniffled, trying to stop the burning in her nose and eyes. "Yeah."

He leaned over, bracing his hands against his knees. "Shit. Why didn't I think of that before? The time machine was the spindle, that's why you traveled in time when you touched it. Your dreams, where you can stop time and change the events. Odin and Thor, I never heard of Norns having children, never thought they could..."

She nodded and looked out to the sea again. "I know. I know. I should think about how to use this knowledge to understand my gift better and to help with Ragnarök... The völva did say I could save the world." Her throat contracted. "But all I can think of"—her jaw tensed as she forced herself to keep back the emotion—"is that my mom never abandoned me because she didn't want me or because something was wrong with me..."

He strode over to face her and wrapped his arms around her, engulfing her in his arms, big and hard and reassuring.

"...but because she isn't even human. Channing, I don't even know exactly why she left. I guess maybe Norns aren't supposed to have children or be married to humans..."

He kissed the top of her head. "I guess not, sweetheart. Her leaving was never about you."

The ball of emotion she kept in her heart exploded, and she

turned to him, burying her face in his chest. It was liberating and sweet and so difficult... She cried into his coat, soft and warm and safe in his hug. She didn't understand what any of it meant. But the man she loved was still here by her side, shielding her from everything.

When she didn't have any tears left to cry, and his lips still pressed against the crown of her head, he said, "That's where your gift comes from."

She looked up at him. His beard had grown over the weeks they'd been in the Viking Age, his skin had become reddened and weathered, and she wondered how she looked herself after so much time spent outdoors in the elements. No moisturizers and vitamin supplements back in the ninth century.

She loved him even more this way. Real. Raw. Every artificial thing and mask stripped away. Just the man she loved, the man she admired, the man she'd said she'd marry.

"Yes," she said. "That's where my ability to manipulate time comes from."

He looked around. "Did you notice? No snow. It's warm, I'm burning in this coat. No wolves... Maybe we escaped Ragnarök. Maybe all that prophecy was left behind. Maybe you wiped the prophecy clean. You might have powers like that if you're part Norn."

She looked around, too. In the distance, cars whirred, and a ship honked its long call. It was hard to say, of course, but everything seemed so peaceful and calm from here, she wanted to believe he was right. She wanted to believe they could finally find the future they could be happy in.

He cupped her jaw and smiled at her. "You're my miracle."

She felt a blush burn her cheeks. "You're just saying that because I can do stuff."

"You've always been my miracle. Before I knew you had any powers. Thank you for saving my life."

He leaned down and kissed her, and she was lost in the warmth and the softness of his lips, the feel of his tongue stroking her gently. Just as she was about to suggest they get out of there, a rooster crowed. Then another. Then a third.

Channing froze and pulled back, looked around. "No."

Her blood chilled. *Three roosters—one crimson, one golden, and one dark red—would crow, calling Ragnarök.*

"No..." she whispered. "God, please, no!"

A wolf howled. An icy gust of wind from the east hit her whole body, making her shrink and shiver. Right on the horizon, where a few moments ago there had been nothing but a dreamy blue sky, a stormy, almost black cloud hung, and waves rose across the whole ocean, as far as she could see. Ravens squawked over their heads, the urgency of their calls signaling trouble.

"No..." Channing echoed, his gaze on the dark and haunted horizon.

"What are we going to do?" she whispered. "How do we stop this?"

He looked back at the rows of the warehouse buildings lining the port roads. "If the time machine was what started this, then we must destroy it."

"But then you won't be able to return to your family."

He gazed at her. "I have you, my love. I don't need to go anywhere as long as I'm by your side."

She choked from the emotion in his eyes. There he was, the end of the world in human form. Not just *the* world...*her* world.

The man holding her heart in his bare hands, owning it, having complete power over it.

And she couldn't do a thing to stop him.

Because she loved him and would rather see the world burn than him.

Something within her told her to stop, to think about what she was doing. Now that she had the power, now that she knew who she really was, she should use it... To protect her family, to save them and the world.

But how? And if she needed to choose between the destiny of the world and the life of the man she loved... Would she be able to make the most difficult choice imaginable?

Selfishly, she ignored the whisper at the back of her mind, the black cloud closing over Boston like a blanket, and the roosters crowing and the wolves howling closer and closer.

She was half Norn. Her mother was one of the three most powerful beings in the whole world, beings feared not just by humans but by the gods themselves. That blood flowed in her veins, and, just like the völva said, that should count for something.

Letting the world around them fade away, she kissed him, a gentle peck on the lips. "Let's go and figure something out."

As they walked towards building M05, memories swarmed into her head. Her meeting Channing near here, her following him, all the questions she had had about that building, and how right she was. Her dad...oh, he must be worried, and Gloria and Ted...

Whatever awaited her and Channing, she felt stronger and more powerful than ever before.

Just imagine, she mentally whispered to herself, *I am half Norn!* She needed to ask her dad everything about her mom... every detail of how they met and how their relationship evolved.

She and Channing had just walked from behind a corner of stacked shipping containers when a hundred feet ahead of them, across the road, three black SUVs pulled up and stopped in front of building M05.

Channing pulled her to the side and behind a dark-red

container. They plastered themselves to the corrugated metal wall of the container and peered around the corner. Two men with assault rifles walked out of building Mo5. They were in black suits and wore dark winter jackets. As they stopped and scanned the surroundings, one of them spoke into his sleeve. The door to Mo5 opened and someone walked out.

A tall older man with long, silvery hair, high cheekbones, and an attractive face. She knew that face.

"Wait...is that Leo Esposito?" Ella whispered.

The head of the Boston Mafia who had bailed Channing out when she'd arrested him. Channing didn't reply for a moment, and when she turned to him, he was ashen. "That's him."

She looked around. "Where are the police? Building Mo5 has to be under police supervision." XXX

Channing spat out an oath. "I don't think the police are in control anymore..."

The door behind Leo opened again and two more men pushed two people in white lab coats in front of them.

"Isn't that...?"

"Odin's rotten cock... They got Georgina and Munchie!"

"Which means..." Ella watched Leo climb into the second black SUV and the two scientists being pushed into the third car.

"The Mafia must have control of the time machine."

"And the reactor."

She looked at him, cold realization crawling over her whole body like icy fog.

Once the other two men climbed into the SUV, the whole procession drove down the street and out of the port.

"We have to do something," Channing growled. "Rescue them. Their lives are probably in danger... And the time machine can't fall into the hands of the Mafia."

Ella searched within herself, trying to do whatever she had done the last time, but nothing happened.

Channing walked out from behind the storage container and stood watching as the SUVs disappeared in the distance. "Goddamn it. Just imagine what they could do. Maybe this is how Ragnarök really will happen. Because if the Mafia is planning to use this power, it can't be for good."

Ella stared after the cars. As the ravens squawked even louder, and the wolves came and surrounded Channing, she realized, no matter how strong and powerful she felt, she didn't know much. There were more powerful enemies at play.

And the biggest battle was still before them.

THANK you for reading AGE OF ICE. I hope you loved the twists and turns of Channing and Ella's story. Find out how their story ends in AGE OF FIRE.

Read AGE OF FIRE now >

☆☆☆☆☆ "The perfect end to the series. Fast-paced, steamy, and full of twists and turns!"

SIGN-UP FOR MY NEWSLETTER to find out when new books release, hear about exclusive giveaways, and take a sneak peek into my future books.

FANCY A HIGHLANDER?

And other mysterious matchmakers are sending people to the Highlands, too. If you haven't read Craig and Amy's story yet, be sure to pick up HIGHLANDER'S CAPTIVE.

In her arms he finds strength. In his arms she finds hope. Can their love outlast the ages?

READ HIGHLANDER'S CAPTIVE now >
⭐⭐⭐⭐⭐ "One of the MOST ROMANTIC AND HEART-WRENCHING TALES I've read in a long while! Absolutely loved it!"

OR STAY with Channing's and Ella's story and keep reading for an excerpt from AGE OF FIRE, the final book in the FATED Series.

HOLDING ELLA'S HAND, Channing walked through a white blizzard. It felt like they were the only people left in the whole world.

Dark shapes of triple-deckers greyed on both sides of the street, but there were no lights in the windows. No music played, no neighbors quarrelled and no dogs barked. A single street light flickered through the curtain of swirling snow.

Only a few weeks ago, Channing had invited himself to a shepherd's pie dinner at the O'Connor family's home. His chest had ached then, thinking of what he had missed. This was a street where neighbors were friendly, children grew up together and you couldn't take a step without someone knowing. This was a street where people were wary of strangers and held tightly to each other. Like the Viking world he'd just left behind.

Like his own family.

Now, it looked like Ragnarök was not just happening but had already ended. And this was afterward.

Where had Dorchester Street gone? It had vanished with the rest of the world. Nothing would ever be the same.

And he was still from nowhere and had no home but this woman walking next to him. The woman who made his blood sizzle. The woman who brought the warmth of an open hearth right into the emptiness in his chest.

"Power must be out," Ella said, raising her voice over the howling wind.

He knew what she worried about. His family was in the Viking Age. Hers was here...but were they okay? He wished he could ease her worry, shield her from everything. Wrap her in a protective cocoon.

He would die for her if he had to.

But was he ready to die for the world?

"We need to hurry, sweetheart," said Channing. "The storm is getting worse."

They sped up.

They had gotten a lift from the Port of Boston and the driver had let them out a few blocks away. The street was impassable except on foot.

When they had left the port, with a sinking, cold desperation Channing had realized the roads were almost car-less. They'd walked south along Summer Street, where a few cars passed but never stopped. Most of the cars still running were electric. With the storms interfering with supply lines, the gas shortage was palpable.

Given their odd Viking clothes, Channing wasn't surprised no one would stop no matter how much they waved their arms. They carried no modern money, no credit cards and no IDs. Their only possession in the world was the Viking travel backpack on Channing's back.

When they'd reached Dorchester Street, a driver had finally stopped. He'd agreed to give them a lift without payment, mumbling something about helping the homeless. About how the end of the world would reveal who we really are.

As they'd driven through South Boston, the car barely fit through the narrow streets. Ragnarök had made snowdrifts out of the parked cars. Rows of triple-deckers had flashed by, dark and lifeless. Bay windows and entrance doors of several were smashed. No children played on the streets. No dogs barked. No birds sang. The few gas stations they passed stood empty, prices for gas having increased tenfold. The driver told them power was out at least once a day now.

How was this better than the Viking Age? They had left his wounded father in the ninth century... Would his mother be able to save him from the gunshot wound? Would they defeat King Harald and his warriors, take back the singed mead hall and get Hakon back on his feet?

Thoughts of his family were like knives slicing through the scabs of a wound that had never fully healed. Ella's hand in his soothed him like a cool balm. He'd lost his family, but she would find hers, and that was worth everything. Because her joy, her happiness was all he cared about.

"Do you even recognize any of the houses?" he asked, blinking fat, weightless snowflakes away.

"I think so," Ella said as she held back the edge of her white fur hood to look to her left. "Main thing is that I don't walk right past my house."

Snow was everywhere, in his eyes and his neck, and his nose. Wind stole his breath as it threw harsh gusts into his face.

Despite the snow and the silence, the thing that most concerned him was that they'd landed in a time where his port had been taken over by the mafia, which told him two things.

Number one, the police were weak enough to have let that happened. Number two, drugs would now flow freely into the city. Those shipments that made it through the storms, which would be even worse in the open seas, anyways.

Which meant, there'd be more crime. The police would be helpless, if they weren't already.

Brothers killing brothers.

Fathers and sons' kinship bonds collapse.

More deaths.

Ragnarök was winning.

For a split second, he remembered the unforgiving, icy cold feel of the wooden stump pressed against his cheek. The sharp edge of the executioner's ax was about to fall.

That would have been it. At any moment, he'd have gone into the great unknown. Would it be Valhalla or something else?

And in those last moments, his life hadn't flashed before his eyes. He hadn't thought of what he should have done differently, of how to fight the two Vikings holding him down.

He'd seen one face in his mind's eye. Icy blue eyes under long, dark-blond eyelashes. Her laughing, white teeth flashing as her pink lips curved up in a smile. How truly beautiful she was, and how lucky he'd been to have had her in his life, by his side.

And he'd wanted more. More time with her. More hand-holding. More kisses. More sex.

More everything.

He'd searched the white space infested by the enemies that had surrounded him in the circle. He wanted to be looking at her in his last moment.

There he'd been, trapped between love and death, the moment stretching like an eternity.

Submitting to what someone else thought was his destiny

went against his nature. But a small part of him knew he should have just accepted his fate then. King Harald wanted to save the world by relieving Channing of it.

That would have been better for everyone.

Only, Ella hadn't let him.

One moment, Channing had seen her, trapped in the arms of King Harald. The next, she wasn't there. Someone had touched him, and he'd been sucked in into a dark nothingness. And then he'd opened his eyes in the Port of Boston.

And he was alive. But should he be?

"There." She tugged him to her left, towards a bright orange and green spot behind the curtain of snow — a building.

The stairs of the front porch were a snowdrift, and they dug their shoes into the snow so as not to slip and fall. The windows were dark. Not surprisingly, the bell didn't work. Ella banged on the front door. No one answered.

"There are emergency generators in my building." Channing stepped up next to her and pounded on the door with his fist. "We're taking them to my apartment."

His apartment, at the top of the fifty-five-floor Millennium Tower, high above the Boston chaos, would be a fortress. No one would break in, and it would stay warm and there'd be light as long as the emergency generators worked. And they were geared for situations like this—that had been one of his requirements when he'd had the tower built.

The violent, rough Viking Age with its wooden longhouses, thatched roofs, and central hearths were one extreme. A cold, creaking triple-decker with no power was another.

"The port is not yours anymore," Ella mumbled, "who's to say your apartment is?"

A THICK, cold silence followed her question. Channing must be contemplating the possibility of having lost both his business and his home. Maybe she shouldn't have brought it up.

In the quiet, she strained her ears, trying to catch a shuffle of feet from behind the front door, a click of the deadbolt being unlatched.

When steps sounded in the foyer, the world gained color. It must be Gloria. The steps were too heavy for Ted, and Dad was in a wheelchair. The peephole darkened for a moment, then nothing. On the tiny, convex circle of glass, Ella watched the two compacted and curved figures in Viking fur cloaks, covered in snow, trails of steam rushing out of their mouths.

"It's me!" she called.

The door flew open, and a white-faced Gloria stood in the frame. Two sweaters hugged her plump, short frame. Her brown hair was messy, so unlike her, as though she hadn't brushed it for days. Winter boots on her feet and a beanie on her head, condensation pumped out of her mouth in small, erratic clouds.

Gloria gave out a high-pitched "Oh!" and hung on Ella's neck, her back shaking as she sobbed. Ella hugged her back and Gloria felt smaller, more delicate under Ella's palms, fragile like a doll.

And for the first time in her life the words, "I'm back, Mom," were born in her throat.

She buried them deep down like she buried her face in Gloria's sweater, the wool scratchy against her cheek. She inhaled the familiar scent of old wood and a whiff of fried onions and garlic. A few moments later, Gloria backed into the dark hall of the triple-decker, wiping her eyes with the backs of her hands. "Come in, come in! Christ on a bike, you're back!"

Ella stepped into the semidark hallway that felt like a tunnel between worlds. Snow blew in after Channing in giant swirls as he followed her. Gloria shut the door behind him, plunging them all into darkness. The scents of a home surrounded her—the chemical smell of cleaning products, the honey-like fragrance of old wood, and the distant scent of a kitchen.

Ella walking briskly towards the gray daylight shining through the apartment door.

She would see her dad and her brother in a moment. Anticipation burned her, the need, the longing for loved ones was like a strong wind pushing her forward.

"Dad!" Ella called. "Ted!"

Inside the apartment, two shadows appeared from the daylight of the living room. Her father, in the wheelchair, and her brother, Ted, a boy of twelve with Down's Syndrome. Ella sank to her knees, hugging Ted first. Bryan caught her hand between his large palms, his skin dry and warm. Ted's eyes were teary, his lips trembling as Ella mumbled she was back, that she was okay, that she'd never leave him again.

As Gloria stepped into the apartment next to Channing and closed the door behind her, Ted grinned, his big eyes wide as he stared at him.

"Did you come with a big boat?" Ted asked him.

Channing grinned back. "Not this time, Ted."

"Hi, Dad," Ella hugged her father and he wrapped his arm around her neck and patted the back of her fur cloak.

Bryan's lips tightened into a firm line as he looked at Channing.

"Thank you for bringing her back to me," he said.

Ella had expected a scowl, some reproach for being the reason his daughter had disappeared in time.

Not a thank you.

"I didn't," Channing said. "It was all her."

Ella straightened up. Relief felt like a tiny sun glowing in her stomach. "Are you guys okay? Dad, have you started the cancer treatments?"

Bryan's face darkened. "We're fine. Come in, both of you. Tell me everything. I'll call Ricardo and you can thank him for getting Hakonson here out of jail."

The house was cold, and Channing suggested that they go to his apartment, but Bryan told him the power would be back on soon.

While Bryan called Ricardo, Gloria brought Ella and Channing two glasses of cold water. It tasted chemical and artificial after the clean mountain water in the Viking Age, and, surprising herself, Ella longed for the warmth of a central hearth and the scent of woodsmoke and Channing's family, fierce and loyal and loving. It would be wonderful to have both families together.

But that was impossible.

When her dad, Gloria and Ted were all present, Ella began telling the story. She kept the most brutal details as general as possible given that her brother was listening. Soon, Ted seemed to lose interest. He asked Gloria to turn on the TV, but when she said the TV didn't work, he asked for his Rolf comic books.

Rolf was a superhero with an ability to throw lightning bolts and an ax that could cut anything. He was probably based on myths about Thor, and Ella wondered distantly how much there was about Ragnarök and about the Norns and the gods in the comic books.

In the middle of her story, a distant banging came from the front door.

Gloria went to open the door and returned accompanied by a crazed-eyed, panting Ricardo.

KEEP READING AGE OF FIRE.

ALSO BY MARIAH STONE

Mariah's Time travel Romance Series

- CALLED BY A HIGHLANDER
- CALLED BY A VIKING
- CALLED BY A PIRATE
- FATED

Mariah's Regency Romance Series

- DUKES AND SECRETS

View all of Mariah's Books in Reading Order

Scan the QR code for the complete list of Mariah's ebooks, paperbacks, and audiobooks in reading order.

GET A FREE MARIAH STONE BOOK!

Join Mariah's mailing list to be the first to know of new releases, free books, special prices, and other author giveaways.

freehistoricalromancebooks.com

ENJOY THE BOOK? YOU CAN MAKE A DIFFERENCE!

Please, leave your honest review for the book.
As much as I'd love to, I don't have financial capacity like New York publishers to run ads in the newspaper or put posters in subway.

But I have something much, much more powerful!

Committed and loyal readers

If you enjoyed the book, I'd be so grateful if you could spend five minutes leaving a review on the book's Amazon page.

Thank you very much!

ABOUT MARIAH STONE

Mariah Stone is a bestselling author of time travel romance novels, including her popular Called by a Highlander series and her hot Viking, Pirate, and Regency novels. With nearly one million books sold, Mariah writes about strong modern-day women falling in love with their soulmates across time. Her books are available worldwide in multiple languages in e-book, print, and audio.

Subscribe to Mariah's newsletter for a free time travel romance book today at mariahstone.com/signup/!

facebook.com/mariahstoneauthor

instagram.com/mariahstoneauthor

bookbub.com/authors/mariah-stone

pinterest.com/mariahstoneauthor

amazon.com/Mariah-Stone/e/B07JVW28PJ